D1168997

PAPER
WORLD

a novel

Maureen
Cummins

PAPER WORLD

© 2021 Maureen Cummins. All rights reserved.

ISBN 978-1-66781-201-4

This is a work of fiction. Names, characters, businesses, places, events, locales, and incidents are either the products of the author's imagination or used in a fictitious manner. Any resemblance to actual persons, living or dead, or actual events is purely coincidental.

No part of this publication may be reproduced, distributed, or transmitted in any form or by any means, including photocopying, recording, or other electronic or mechanical methods, without the prior written permission of the author, except in the case of brief quotations embodied in critical reviews and certain other noncommercial uses permitted by copyright law.

this book is dedicated to the most important people in my life.

to my parents and grandmother,
for showing me what true love means.

to all the men who inspired this story,
for loving me and then breaking my heart.

to my best friend,
for always being there to pick up the pieces.

and to my husband,
for putting those pieces back together.

"It was like when you ripped a piece of paper into two:
no matter how you tried, the seams never fit exactly right again."

-Sarah Dessen
What Happened to Goodbye

Fading.
       A door
       creaks.

A thud.
       Two hands
       cradle the sides of my face.

       Then,
       darkness.

A QUESTION

It's all a blur to me now.

I know I'm still alive, but it doesn't feel that way. How did I get here? In this cold, painfully bright room. I can't open my eyes, but the fluorescent lights permeate my eyelids, flushing my brain with a debilitating glow. I am freezing, but my skin feels like it's been flayed. On fire, almost.

Strange.

I picture what that might look like, my outer layer peeled back. An image of myself in the most candid detail. Like my sixth-grade biology textbook come to life. I try to take a breath, at least, I think that I do. But there is something stopping this natural impulse. If I hadn't overheard someone mention quietly that I seem to be adjusting well to my intubation, I may not have even realized: I'm in a hospital, and I am on life support.

Growing up, I had always felt that there was this incredibly complex mix of emotions that a hospital could make someone feel. My dad was a bit of a nervous parent, and the emergency room always seemed to be the obvious answer to the most trivial of childhood injuries. I still remember the sheer panic I felt the day that I was bitten by a spider, and my father whisked me away in our off-white family caravan to the Arnold Palmer

1

Memorial Hospital down the road. Sometimes I think we moved to our mid-sized, lakeside home because of its proximity to the emergency room. I recall him carrying me through those revolving glass doors, holding me akin to a gunshot victim, demanding that a doctor see his baby girl right away. Terrifying for any child, that fear in their parents' eyes.

But the anxiety I felt at seeing my father fall to pieces with stress seemed to melt away when I was placed in that hospital bed. The fresh, newly washed sheets, those clean, white walls and that expensive, shiny equipment: it was all there to make me feel better. And my world slowed down. I felt protected. Like there was nothing I couldn't survive as long as I ended up in that glistening, polished room.

But here I am, twenty-six years old, and I am not safe. I am dying, and the worst part is: I have no idea how I got here.

CHAPTER 1

My twenty-sixth year started out like every other was meant to after the twenty-first: entirely uneventful. I had a cake. My parents sang me "Happy Birthday" at a nice restaurant. I opened presents. One truly signified a mid-twenties birthday: fun socks. Flamingos drinking margaritas. Why had I been getting more of these lately? I was at least thankful that I lived in Orlando where I could celebrate with either a fancy dinner near the theme parks or a wild night chugging shitty beer in dank downtown bars. The latter was entirely unappealing to me this year. There is just something about celebrating another trip around the sun that becomes progressively less exciting after the legal drinking one. And, man, after twenty-five? There is really nothing to celebrate. Well, except for a discovery that most liquors now cause massive hangovers and that being able to legally rent a car is a useless milestone.

But, when I thought about it, I actually did have some mature life experiences to celebrate. Landmarks, if you will. Benchmarks. I was engaged to my college sweetheart, and it was right on schedule. Less than a year before, on Valentine's Day and right before my twenty-fifth birthday, he got down on one knee and promised to love me for the rest of our lives. Well, that might have been what he said. In truth, I was too overwhelmed by the moment that I had been waiting for since birth to ensure I took part in my only part of the process: remembering it. And say yes. Did I even do that?

They say that some of life's happiest moments, engagement included, are a total blur. A mix of adrenaline and excitement stops the usual firing of neurons. Your brain ceases to absorb the memories. Like it's so overwhelmed with bliss that it can't do anything but live in that exact moment. You're robbed, in a way. Required to constantly be aware of the *now*. In truth, I guess I never learned to live in the moment. But I like to think that was how we lived our relationship in the beginning, Kurt and me.

Kurt.

Our love story started off in many ways, standard. We went to the same high school in Orlando, though we never officially met there. Different circles. We wound up at the same college, Florida State University. By then, we had friends in common. We started dating. And then, well, we just stayed together. And five years later, Kurt got down on one knee. For the life of me, I couldn't remember what he said. What were his promises to me? There were mornings that I would take out a pen and paper and beg my mind to send me back to that moment and let me relive that happiness. I never got my wish. So, it goes.

After I blew out the big candles labeled 'two' and 'six' (so no one would forget which birthday we were celebrating), I felt a kiss on my right cheek. Soft, calm. A flash went off. My parents have a camera, I gathered.

"Happy birthday, Brett."

"Thanks, babe. Hopefully it's not true what they say, that your looks start to fade after twenty-six."

I was not exactly a fan of the idea of growing older. What woman is? I knew that it came with its benefits: maturity, wisdom and a grounding sense of self-awareness. You came into your own, no longer relying on what others thought to shape your idea of significance. It also came with its pitfalls: decline in looks and virility, a foreboding sense of death's knock reaching closer and closer to your own door. A downward spiral, if you will. To add insult to injury, I was a year older than Kurt. That rarely bothered me. It's not like I ever noticed it when we were together. But I'd read online somewhere that a woman reaches her peak, physically, in her twenty-sixth year. Something about her features all finally working together, like a seamlessly written symphony which has taken decades to perfect.

Blowing out my brightly illuminated candles, I made a pact with the universe. I asked whatever it was in charge of the Earth, be it one merciful God, many critical gods, or the devil himself: let my youth last a bit longer. I wanted to stay twenty-six eternally. Forever young. How Dorian Gray of me. How could *that* go wrong? And, really, what a selfish wish. Who cared if I was growing older, as long as my life was progressing upward? It was the way existence worked. But I wasn't ready to start my decline. I would tuck my portrait away, bowels of the closet, and let it rot.

Watching my cake being cut by our server, a gorgeous girl who must have still been in high school, I considered how men aged so gracefully in comparison to women. I looked over at Kurt and realized just how true that was. So striking. He still made me swoon. Even after five years together, I never took for granted how handsome he was.

I remember the night we officially met. A mutual friend introduced us one weeknight. We were at a tea shop that had been a campus staple for over a decade. It had recently made the conversion into a hookah-lounge at night. How very 2010 that transformation was: students could grab a tea on the way to their modern art class and end their studious days with an hour puffing on a shared Middle Eastern tobacco pipe.

I recognized Kurt the moment he walked through that wooden door with its creaky, slanting panels. He was the kid with the perfect, wispy, auburn hair from our high school soccer team. The kind of guy you'd find on an Abercrombie and Fitch shopping bag in the early 2000s. I was such a sucker for that look. I followed him with my eyes until he sat down at our table, across from me but close enough that I could smell his cologne. When he finally smiled at me and introduced himself, I nearly melted. Kind, green eyes that betrayed his every thought. A wide smile that was completely approachable. And, oh, a laugh that was so pure, you couldn't hear it without feeling lighter. I was in over my head.

"Hey, I know you! We went to the same high school – you ran cross country, right?" he said, pointing a finger in my direction.

Internal scream. He remembered me.

"Yeah, we did! Go Hornets!" Did I really say that? How entirely lame of me. Get it together, I said to myself. "But, um, yeah, I did run, were you on the team? I don't think I remember you?"

Better.

Play it off like you didn't stare at him every time he passed you in the halls.

Less creepy this way.

Keep it up, Brett, I told myself with a psychological pat on the back.

"Oh, no I played soccer. But my best friend over here, Jay, was on the team." He nodded to the guy sitting next to him.

"Yeah, you were fast as hell," his friend said. I remembered Jay. Short with brown hair and freckles, he was a shy kid. Had a lot of siblings.

"Yeah, he said you're not bad with a beer bong either," Kurt added. He broke a smile.

Well, let's hope he doesn't know too much. Cross country parties were not where I was at my best, historically speaking. One particular party I wound up streaking. I never was able to turn down a dare.

"Ah, well, my reputation precedes me. One is a little more impressive than the other, I guess? I'm Brett," I said, taking a sip of my boba tea.

"Kurt. Brett, yeah, I always wondered about your name. I have a cousin, Brett, but he definitely doesn't look as good in a dress. Is that a family name?" asked Kurt. Jay quietly chuckled next to him.

I smiled with my lips still hovering over my drink. Funny and he paid me a compliment. In that moment, even at twenty years old, I felt like I was still the awkward girl in middle school who couldn't talk to a cute

6

boy without stumbling over her every word. A flashback to pre-pubescent school dances and sitting alone on the bleachers. I forced myself to make eye contact with him.

"Well, yeah, I mean... it's from *The Sun Also Rises*. My parents were big fans of Hemingway. I guess I kind of followed in their footsteps, I'm an English major," I said, hoping he found me cute and not just a book nerd, which I was.

I have never been without a book in my hands. My parents owned a restaurant that doubled as a bookshop for most of my growing years. I spent every day surrounded by volumes. They were often too busy to entertain me themselves. They left that up to the books. I was fascinated by Shakespeare at the age of eight. I likened myself to Juliet and expected to one day find my Romeo. Clearly, I was too young to understand the theme of that tragedy. All I saw were the beautifully crafted devotional couplets. I wanted a boy to love me that way.

"That's awesome! I like to write, but I'm no Hemingway. If you're a big reader, too, maybe I could show you some of my stuff? I'm an Economics major so I'm definitely no grammar whiz," he said, pushing his long, auburn locks to the side of his lightly freckled face. He wrote, too? Oh man, was I swooning.

And then we talked about books and all things literature for hours. He was a fan of both fantasy and poetry. I was a true devotee of the classics. But we both had immense respect for any writing, really. That was the key. At one point, we were comparing *Lord of the Rings* and *Atlas Shrugged*. We agreed that an author who could form captivating fictional realms from scratch was just as talented as one who could make a reader see our already existing society in a unique light. I was in love with him by the time we exchanged numbers. After a hug that lingered almost as long as I'd wanted it to, we went our separate ways for the night. He had an air about him that, to me, was powerful—and I would have sat at that table with him forever.

And, as it would turn out, I was still sitting across from him at a table, five years later. He never did show me his writings. In truth, I never asked. I'm not sure if I had given the impression that I didn't care; nothing could have been further from the truth. Over the years, Kurt had become a lot more private with his thoughts. Guarded, even. Those kind eyes no longer held his deepest feelings in two pools of tranquil green. I never did discover what altered that in him. It was as if the transformation was a natural one, like life had come along and wrapped him into itself, a cocoon, causing him to emerge a more restrained human being.

There was *something* a bit off with him lately. He was quieter than usual. I guess, in truth, that wasn't too surprising, considering. Jay had recently disappeared. One morning his roommate went into his room to borrow his computer, and it was gone. Jay was gone. He had taken everything of importance with him. Evidently, that wasn't too much. Most of his room was left untouched. Apparently, he had suffered a sort of psychedelic-caused meltdown. Drug-induced psychosis, Kurt would correct me. He had been using mushrooms as a means of connecting more closely with his inner self. LSD, too. I guess he didn't like what he found.

He left notes to his parents and one of his sisters, asking them not to come after him. He also left one for Kurt. Kurt said that the note stated that he had left on a bus and was bound for a small town in Colorado. That he would find a job planting trees there. Kurt refused to disclose anything else and asked me not to read the note. I wasn't sure why I couldn't see what he wrote, but I obliged, it was not my place. Jay also left a sort of stoner's manifesto on his desk. His roommate said it was mostly incoherent ramblings about feeling like a lone wolf.

No one had heard from him, and it had been about a week.

Kurt took that really hard. It made sense: after all these years, Jay was still his very best friend. He was even supposed to be his best man in our wedding. How cruel, I thought, to leave Kurt like that. But I wouldn't have known any of this from Kurt explaining it to me: in all our years together, I was never able to get any emotional read on him. He was a closed book when it came to his feelings. The only reason I knew he was struggling with Jay's absence was because of how often he stole away to write. He had a notebook, leather-bound and the color of deep, weathered wood, that was his sanctuary. He had it for as long as I'd known him. Kurt never went anywhere without his "paper world" as he deemed it, and it was one of the most beautiful qualities about him. I loved this man for many reasons, but as an avid reader, this was something about him I worshipped. It was okay that he didn't let me in. He was a writer. He just saved his thoughts for paper.

I knew that after dinner with my parents, we had a ritual that we would need to complete once we walked into our home. It consisted of a bottle of wine, always a Shiraz and always Australian, and a healthy-sized bowl of weed. After a few years together, we matured in our choice of drink, but we never did give up our college-born reliance on marijuana. I learned the night of our first meeting that neither one of us liked smoking hookah, a trend which had recently boomed with university students. Tobacco always seemed to make me feel like my head was swimming in a choppy ocean while my body was crumbling on a planet with a massive gravitational pull. And after we both passed on the hookah when it came to our turns, I learned that Kurt was just as keen on weed as me.

As most seemingly destructive relationships go, we founded our relationship on a mutual desire to be high. We didn't have too much in common, it turned out, but we did have that. We mistook escaping life's difficulties for a love of red-eyed laughter and late-night snacks. And we built a relationship on that talent for avoidance. I knew that after all these years, we should have had another way to manage stress. Find shared interests that didn't involve intoxication. But it worked for us. And I loved him. I knew that Kurt was hurting, and I knew that a Band-Aid fix was all I could do for him then. He missed his friend, and I wasn't going to get much more from him than that. So, dinner ended, and I kissed my mom and dad goodbye, thanked them for an amazing dinner, stuffed the bird-covered socks in my purse, and walked, hand in hand with Kurt, to my car.

On my once free ring finger sat a diamond. It felt like it had always been there, in a way. I couldn't help but admire its shine as I used my hand to open the car door and slide into the passenger seat next to my soon-to-be husband. In just two months, I would be his wife, and my life would be exactly where I wanted it to be. Everything moving on schedule. He was quiet on the ride home, but that wasn't uncommon, especially lately. And it didn't bother me, because I was already absorbed with mentally checking off that everything still needed completing for the big day. Kurt wasn't really into wedding planning from the start, he let me take the lead on most of the decisions. But that was okay with me: I wasn't a natural planner, but this was our wedding day and I was up for the task. My mind was on seating arrangements when we pulled up to our humble abode.

Before we got out of the car, I paused upon seeing our house. It was, to be blunt, a shack. After graduating college, neither one of us had a prestigious job that paid the bills. I worked for a local book publisher, editing other people's dreams, while still trying to write my own. I had been dabbling in short stories for a while, and my after-work hours consisted of penning my thoughts to paper and then typing them up on my computer to be sent off to a number of online publishers, never to be given the answer I so craved: "yes, we will publish your work." I wanted so badly for my words to line the minds of others, just as classic quotes in literature never seemed to escape mine. Though Kurt also had a talent for writing, he graduated with a major in Microeconomics. However, he had trouble finding any jobs that required his specific expertise, and had only been able to find work with local construction companies. He discovered that he liked working with his hands and began frequently informing me that bachelor's degrees are for chumps. I didn't agree and informed him that our future children would still be attending college. He never argued that. So, we were receiving minimum wage bi-weekly checks and our home reflected that.

As frustrating as that was for us at the time, I was overcome with the feeling that one day, when we were sixty and living in the home of our dreams on the water, we would look back on this period of our lives and this house and be filled with a feeling of gratitude. We would remember this home, and smile. We would think back on our first day in our new house. The first time we stepped through its wonky door frame, the one we fixed by ourselves. We would remember painting the stained, spider-web covered walls, and leaving each other little love letters with colour. We would reminisce on our first night, sitting on flattened cardboard boxes, lighting candles and eating Chinese food. How we laid our heads down in sleeping bags because we hadn't been able to buy ourselves a bed just yet. The light kisses he gave me while I was wrapped in his arms. Kurt and I would recall this house with warm smiles; because it was ours, and because we had truly loved one another within its four walls.

After a few years of living in it, unlocking our front door and walking into our house had a different feel to it. It had become more of a home in the traditional sense. There was furniture, and we had a bed. We used dishes to hold our food and silverware while we ate it. The walls were not only covered in paint, but also adorned with pictures. Pictures of us. Our little shack had come to house our life together and I felt that it was a perfect start. And so on the night of my twenty-sixth birthday, my mind was ablaze with memories of my life with Kurt. Where we had been, where we were now, and where we were going, together. I followed Kurt to our kitchen table, seemingly walking on air. I had been so consumed with thoughts of how perfect my life would be, that I didn't recognize the wreckage that it already was. I heard him speak.

"Brett, we need to talk."

CHAPTER 2

n the history of human interaction, there has never been a good ending to "we need to talk." The phrase reverberated in my ears like a clash of thunder on a tranquil night. Where did it come from? I was stunned, as if a bolt of lightning had let loose from the unexpected storm. Did I hear that right? I may not have remembered what he said when he proposed, but I would never forget the words that came after that phrase.

"Look, Brett, there is no easy way to say this—"

"Say what, Kurt?" I asked, standing up from the table.

I had to keep my hands on it to stay upright.

What the hell was going on?

"I love you, Brett, you know that I do. I mean, we've been together since we were kids. We were teenagers when we met. But maybe that's part of the problem. We don't know anything else."

"Hold on, are you…you're breaking up with me? Is that…wait."

I was dumbfounded.

Speechless.

I looked at him.

He stared back at me.

He's calm.

Why was he so calm?

"It's," he blinked, "I think I am."

A pause.
My eyes refocused.
I stared at the breaks in the wooden table.
I needed a moment.
Was this happening?
But I needed to order table linens.
He spoke again.

"We've only ever known each other, right? That can't be *normal*, you know? We haven't seen…we don't know what else is out there."
"I'm sorry, are you breaking up with me…because you want to fuck other women?"

Wait a minute.
So, he *was* breaking up with me.
I wasn't enough?

"No, that's not…that's not what I'm saying…" He struggled to find words.

He started pacing.
My eyes followed his rapid movement.
Quick.
Flighty.
A bird locked in a cage.
He was searching for his exit.
Did he want me to *give* him one?
Now I was mad.

"Okay, so what *are* you saying?! Fucking say what you're trying to say to me because right now…I'm not fully understanding, Kurt."

I moved toward the kitchen to fill my glass.

Red.

Australian.

Shiraz.

"Look, our relationship hasn't been the same for a while. You have to have noticed that. We haven't been us in so long. I thought it was being comfortable, but I realized it's just… growing apart."

At that last statement, I felt like I'd been gutted. Growing apart? What did he mean? We are *comfortable*. What's wrong with that? I turned to look into his eyes, mine afire with confusion, sadness, betrayal. I had never felt so much in so little time. But when my eyes connected with his, as they had so many times before, all I saw in them was apathy. Like he had just told me that the weather had looked like rain tonight, and not that he wanted to end our relationship.

"I don't … I'm trying to wrap my head around this, Kurt. What the hell are you talking about? Where is this coming from? When did we become… not us?" I asked, using every ounce of my strength to stifle back angry tears.

"Brett, I'm so sorry. I don't know how to explain this to you. I don't want to hurt you, that is the last thing I want."

"Well," I said in a gasp of pain, "you're not exactly doing a great job of that right now."

"*Fuck*, okay," he said while rubbing his face with the palms of his hands. "But, really, Brett, this *can't* be a total surprise to you. Think about the last few months. What in the last few months has been healthy about us?"

But when I thought about it, we had been good. Calm, even. We hadn't been fighting. In fact, we actually hadn't raised our voices at each other in a long time. We had a history of arguing in college and sometimes that turned into full-fledged fights. But we had always forgiven each other with as much vigor as we showed when we fought, and our make-up sex was never short of electric. That was when I realized I couldn't remember our last fight, and I definitely couldn't remember the last time that we had sex. I couldn't remember the last time we…felt. Still, it was all meant to stay on schedule. We were meant to stay on schedule.

"Kurt. We're supposed to get married in two months. I sent out our fucking *wedding* invitations last week! I cannot believe this."

It was all crashing down.
Crumbling, and I couldn't hold it up.
Not by myself.
The harder I tried, the more it would weigh.
Was I meant to shrug it all off?

"I get that, I do."

The irony in those last two words really hit me like a brick wall.
I do.

"Do you? Because my bachelorette was supposed to be next weekend. I mean, *fuck!*"

Upon crying out that last word, I slammed my fist on the table and the wine glass crashed to the floor. The sound of it was followed by a stillness that we soaked in, just for a moment. It was like the house had called a 'time-out' on us both. Like it was asking us to *really* think about what we were going to say to each other next. Kurt sighed. The air he drew in was quick and sharp, and the breath that he let out contained all the fight that he had left. What was left was a man devoid of feeling.

Was I meant to shrug now?

15

"I think that when we sent out those invitations, that was the moment that I knew. It kind of hit me when I saw the look on your face. You were so excited, Brett, and I just… I couldn't match that. I felt…nothing. And I fucking *hated* myself for it." He turned away to avoid seeing the look of pain on my face.

Planning this wedding had been my entire life this past year, and I couldn't imagine not walking down that aisle in May. In that moment, a thought crept into my mind, slowly and diabolically, as did the wedge in our relationship. He was right. This was not a total surprise. But I wasn't giving up that easily. I was panicking, and I couldn't imagine my life without him. I wasn't letting him go without a fight. Even if our relationship didn't deserve that salvation. Even if it was a Band-Aid fix on a much, much bigger wound.

"Look, Kurt, you don't have do this. We can figure it out, okay?! Whatever is going on with us that is broken, we can fix it! I can't imagine my life without you. Please, Kurt, please! We can *fix* it…"

I knew that I was begging, but I couldn't stop myself.

The tears were flowing, and they weren't angry anymore.

They were just desperate.

"Brett, I just… I know that something here isn't right. *We* aren't right. I don't think this is something we can just *fix*."

He said the last word so quietly, I saw his exhaustion as an invitation to change his mind.

"But we can! We've fixed us before, Kurt! How many times have we had shitty moments where we came out stronger! The time I caught you texting your ex when we first started dating? I mean, that could have been the end for us. But instead, we had a deep talk and, Kurt, do you remember? It ended with you calling me your girlfriend for the first time."

"Brett—"

"And do you remember when we first moved in together? That one weekend, I wanted us to drive up to Tally to see everyone and you wanted to stay here. It was such a *stupid* fight, but at the end of it, you told me you were thankful I made us go, you said that I helped you. You said I made you *better*—"

I was sobbing.
In our relationship, I always dove in the water, I guess.
He had always been the one who waded.

"Brett, please, *stop*. I remember all of that."

He turned around and stared at the front door. I silently waited for what I said to matter. It just needed to sink in, the reasons we worked. We made each other *better*. How could he not remember that? I sank back down into my chair at our kitchen table.

"We just…we can't go through with it. *I* can't go through with it, Brett. I'm so, *so* sorry. I can't… I can't marry you."

And in that moment I felt my heart shatter into a million, little pieces. And with every piece that broke off from another, I was torn between two emotions: mourning over a future that I'd never have and anger with myself for not having seen the signs. No matter what I told him, I couldn't convince him that our relationship was capable of the big fix. Not a Band-Aid this time, but a repair that started at the foundation, strengthening the structure as it healed, and coating the walls with a clean, fresh coat of paint. The healthy marriage I had always envisioned would not be built from rusted pipes and broken beams. He was going to leave, and I couldn't stop him from going.

It was time to shrug.

As Kurt moved to leave through our front door with its wonky frame, I stopped for a moment, begging my brain with the last of my strength to at least take this moment in. It wasn't blissful, but it was important. I was watching the love of my life for one last time. He had broken my heart, but I thought if I could just hold onto this moment for a little longer, it would be like withdrawing from happiness instead of losing it cold turkey. I took one last, greedy look. He turned and we looked at one another. Those kind, green eyes locked with mine. Finally, I could see emotion: a mixture of pain and contentment.

"I'll come by tomorrow while you're at work for my things, okay. I really, God… I really am sorry."

Watching him open the door, I spoke one last time.

"Can you at least tell me why? I mean, give me a *real* reason. Something that can help me understand. I just… please. Give me *something*." The last word I said in a near whisper.

"It wouldn't matter, Brett. It wouldn't change anything."

The door closed behind him.
He was gone.
And, in truth, so was I.

CHAPTER 3

E very moment that passed during that night after he left was excruciating. The first hour was spent in silence. I lay slumped by the front door, deflated, like a puppet who had lost its strings. I couldn't bring myself to move. I felt weighted down with the gravity of every sign that I'd missed. Every clear signal that Kurt was unhappy. Any warning that we were doomed. How had I not seen this coming? But I couldn't bear to dissect our relationship just yet.

It wasn't even the bad memories that I wanted to avoid, honestly. I would have welcomed feeling like this was for the best. What I couldn't survive was being swarmed with all the good ones. To think back to those small moments with Kurt that made me feel warm – like the day that we spent at the beach in the heat of the sun on rented scooters, zooming down the loosened sand and racing the incoming tide. We had ended that perfectly golden day with a six-pack of craft beer and sweet public intimacy that may have been illegal. But, damn, it made for one hell of a story at parties. I was proud of that moment and I loved the way that people smiled at us when we giggled at that confession. We couldn't keep our hands off of each other and that kind of tenderness made people jealous. But that story was from the first year that we met and the adventurous, love-soaked piece of us had crashed like the waves.

After what felt like an eternity, I finally pried myself away from the inside of our front door. My two hands beneath me, I hoisted myself up from the floor. One foot in front of the other, feeling heavy, I collapsed onto our bed. My back to the covers, I stared at the ceiling.

"My kitchen table now, my bed," I reminded myself aloud.

This space was no longer shared; it was now mine, and mine alone. That thought was my breaking point, and I desperately searched for my cellphone. I needed to call Phoebe.

Phoebe was my best friend. We met at university and hit it off instantly, paired together in Spanish class and forced to create a disaster of a project together. I spoke Spanish semi-fluently, it was a requirement I take a language at the Catholic school I attended. Even though she did not, lack of knowledge wasn't the issue. We spent most of the time together smoking weed in her hammock instead of working. We got a C+ on that assignment. That day after class, we toasted our semi-passing grade with three pitchers of beer at 2 p.m. We were inseparable ever since.

Since neither one of us had siblings of our own, as time went on we began calling each other "twin." We even looked alike with long, blonde hair that sat wavy when we let it air-dry and piercing blue-green eyes, a shade which could mimic either a calm, cloudless day or a vicious storm on the sea, depending on our moods. Phoebe had been my beacon in life these past eight years. And so once more, I called upon my guiding light to bring me back to shore.

She picked up after one ring.

"Brettttt! Happy birthday, *bitch*! How hammered are you right now – scale of one to ten? Anything less than nine and we've got problems."

Hearing her voice, I immediately began to cry again. The dam I had been keeping closed for the last hour since he left had broken, and an ocean of tears rained into the phone. I tried to speak through the cries. All the words came out broken.

"Brett?! What the hell happened?! Are you okay?! What's going on? Take a breath, talk to me," she said, alarm in her voice.

"He's... gone, Pheebs. He... he left. It... it's over."

Sob after sob.

The pain wasn't stopping, and I couldn't keep it in.

It felt like I was decaying, slowing turning grey, from the inside out.

Like everything would soon turn to ash, and I would blow away with the smallest gust of wind.

"What do you mean? *Who's* gone? Kurt?!" She asked with a slight panic.

"Yeah, Pheebs," I was pulling myself together just enough to try and explain, "he said he doesn't want to get married. And he just... left. I don't know what to do, I feel like I'm in a fucking *nightmare*."

It all hurt too much.

"Okay, okay, *listen* – you are *going* to get through this, Brett. I know it doesn't seem like it right this second, and you probably don't want to hear it but you *will*. Can you tell me what happened?"

"Honestly, I don't think so. Shit, I don't even fucking *know*."

"Well, did he tell you *why*?"

She was a science major. Prescriptive. She needed an answer. Shit, so did I.

"No, Pheebs. I mean, not really. I know about as much as you do, as fucked as that is."

"Jesus, Brett... I am so sorry. I don't know what to say." Her voice wavered. "What can I do?"

"My head hurts, my heart hurts, my fucking *eyes* hurt from crying. I just...wanted to hear your voice. I'm going to drink this bottle of expensive-ass *bullshit* wine that I bought us and go to bed. I'm fine, I just need this night to be over."

I needed to get drunk.

I needed to forget.

Kurt.

"Yeah, I totally understand. For sure, drink that bottle. Shit, drink another one. But I want you to try your best to sleep at least a little bit. Tomorrow morning, I'm driving to you. I'll be there in the afternoon, okay? We can do whatever you want. Cry, scream, eat, get high. Literally *whatever* you want, we can do it. Just get some rest tonight. And if you can't sleep – call me. I mean it, Brett. *Call me."* .

She had always been this friend for me. Always ready to drop anything to be by my side. I'd never known someone so selfless. I knew this would be hard on her, to be comforting me through this. She was friends with Kurt, too. They'd always been pretty close. They used to do mushrooms together in college. On one truly ridiculous trip, they had decided to start a little drug dealing business. It was nothing big time, just weed. It didn't last long, about one month in they realized they were spending more than they were making because they kept giving deep discounts to their friends. I was their delivery girl, and one-hundred percent part of the problem. I would smoke our product with every "client" I visited.

Phoebe always said that we were still her favorite people to spend time with and was quick to accept any invitation to stay at our place. Some of my favorite memories were with both of them next to me. I always counted myself so lucky that they were close, too. It made everything so much easier. But I knew that no matter what, she would feel an allegiance to me at the end of the day. We were sisters. I didn't want to be selfish, but I wanted that. I needed Phoebe to be on my side in all of this.

I promised I would call if the night came to be too much, and she promised to answer if I needed saving. We hung up the phone, and I searched the room for the wine. That annoyingly over-priced bottle I had purchased to celebrate *my own* birthday. Kurt wasn't a big gift-giver, but I had always looked past it. I just assumed he'd been too busy to buy me a present this year, the card I'd received was the best indicator of that possibility. It was the Christmas card he had forgotten to give me the past year.

He had crossed out 'Merry Christmas' and written 'Happy Birthday' over the scratches. I thought it was funny when I had opened it before dinner, so like Kurt to repurpose an abandoned gift. Now, looking at the haphazard writing on this desperate, last-minute excuse for affection, I saw it for what it really was—the perfect symbol of what our relationship had become. Lazy, lost and lifeless.

I grabbed the wine and a bottle opener and sat back down onto the floor. I welcomed the cold sensation of the tiles on my skin. Suddenly, I was on my side, feeling the icy chill of the rock on my cheek. In that moment, I was looking under our bed. My bed. My gaze fell upon that weathered notebook I had seen in my fiancé's arms so many times before.

My ex-fiancé.

A stranger.

I thought about how little I really knew about our relationship; how little I knew about *him*. The man who shared a bed with me for five years. It started to make me feel sick. For how long had he been wanting out of this relationship? Why did he want out of it? How many nights did he lay next to me thinking, "this is not the woman I want to spend my life with"? He never talked to me, he never let me know what he was thinking. He was always just writing.

Writing.

What if that little leather notebook held the answers? Without taking another moment to consider what I was doing it was already in my hands. Feeling the tattered edges, I was comforted. Kurt was in my hands.

I knew that what I was doing was the biggest form of betrayal fathomable. I was, without permission, peering over the enormous walls that Kurt had built from day one around his soul. I figured he had shattered *my* soul and that was without my permission, as well. So, I unfastened the twine that secured its pages, and I opened it. The sensation of the cover on my fingers felt like I had something sacred in my hands—something that would either bless me or curse me with what lie in its pages. Like it housed illicit knowledge, the forbidden fruit. I may be naked for eternity after taking a bite, but I couldn't turn back now. I peeled back the front cover and couldn't believe what I read.

It was incredible. Every single word. Somehow both forceful and delicate. It was like seeing Kurt, really seeing him, for the first time. And that was a magical gift, one I had been craving since the night at that hookah bar. Kurt may not have been able to communicate, verbally, all that he felt. But give that man a pen and he spoke chronicles. His verses could move mountains. And in this wonderfully elusive moment, his words moved me.

The first poem that caught my eye was about his love of escaping the world with whatever book he was devouring most recently. Entitled *Paper World*, the moniker he eventually gave the notebook itself, the poem was strikingly poignant. It was both beautiful and distressing.

paper world

i have read so many books
i have devoured so many words
i have dove into so many worlds.

each time I turn the final page
    -i pause-
    -i feel-
i relish the last moments of total submersion.

because these worlds explored
these lives lived
these tales told
are all a means of escaping my own.

and each time I leave a paper-world
i am sure that I will never detach
my soul from its pages.

with each book I read
i leave a part of myself
within the binding.

    I never knew how hard reality had become for him, or when he had lost the lightness he once possessed. Why was the "real world" so hard to enjoy now? When I met Kurt, I knew he loved to lose himself within a book. I did, too. But he also enjoyed the life that surrounded him. We used to spend summer days at the trails by our student apartment housing, with nothing but a joint and our hiking boots. Some days, we would even leave our phones in the car, just to be that much more removed from society. It would be so overwhelmingly hot that we'd eventually strip down to our bare skin and soak our bones in the cool, cleansing water of the nearest spring. That was how he first got poison ivy, and I found my first tick hitching a ride on my upper thigh.

    I missed those days, and I missed Kurt even more.

    Kurt.

    I turned a few more pages, attempting to soak in every letter, every touch of ink to paper. I yearned to know more about went on in his heart, and in exactly what moment I had left it. I found another one, about halfway through the notebook. And upon reading it, I realized: this one, these words were about me. It was short, but it spoke volumes.

fleeting

they shared their secrets
and their souls
with the fire of the sun

and the calm of the moon
that rested ever so out of reach that night.

but it graced their every movement
with something so pure
he wouldn't give it a name
for fear that it might gain wings
and leave forever.

My heart was so miserably full—it was brief in words, but an epic in emotion. Until this evening, when he told me we were so irreversibly broken, I felt that the most beautiful aspect of our relationship was our ability to say so much without saying anything at all. I knew when I was in his arms that he held me tightly because he loved me, without any words needing to be said. And now I knew that he did so because he was afraid I would one day fly away. He left because he was just scared of having his *own* heart broken. That wasn't something that was unfixable. I could show him that I wouldn't leave. We could stay in the light of the moon, sharing secrets, forever.

Tears pooling in my eyes and silently streaming down my face, I turned another few pages. I had to read more about what he felt in the moments when his lips would not betray him. When his mind retreated as deeply as possible behind those towering, secure walls. I read another poem. This one gave me chills.

truth/lie

people tell a lot
of little white lies.
but this one isn't light.
its dark.

so dark, in fact,
that it steals away
all the beauty
of so many things
you'd told me before.

steals and swallows our memories
and rewrites them with a murky pen.

all because of one truth
that easily could have been a lie.

and we'd all be better for it.

What the hell could that possibly have been about? What lie was Kurt struggling with, and why was the truth so much harder to swallow? I tried to think back to any major life experiences that had thrown him for a loop. I knew he had a rocky relationship with his parents. They were both extremely religious and were overtly displeased with his lifestyle, typical WASPs who drank constantly but turned their noses up to our marijuana use. To add insult to injury, we were living together and unmarried. They wanted us to fit into their box and "living in sin" wasn't acceptable. But they had been so overjoyed to find out we were engaged, and even happier to hear that we had planned on having children. His mother even pulled me aside during Thanksgiving to gently remind me that their table was big enough to pull up another seat. Was this heated poem indicative of some new altercation that I had somehow missed?

A bit more aggressively than I meant it, I turned the pages of his 'paper world'. I ripped the edge of one of the pages. Oh no, *Kurt*. Cursing my panic, I attempted to tend to the tear. On this page, I found another poem he wrote, a bit more recently by its placement in the notebook. I stopped my frantic and entirely useless attempt to fix the page once I read its title. *An Unsent Letter.* It read:

No matter what stretch of time
or distance passes between us,
my heart knows one thing:
no one will ever know my soul
the way that you did.

not a day passes by
that this thought
doesn't cross my mind.
our time can never be erased,
and the imprint you left on me
can never be lessened.

it would be easier if it could be
and I often wish for that relief.
but, as the days draw to a close,
i am constantly left with that same realization:
    you were wholly mine
    and I was wholly yours.

And it was beautiful.

It was a love letter. But it wasn't to me.

CHAPTER 4

S o, there it was. I had bitten the fruit, I had gained the knowledge, and now, I felt entirely naked. Kurt had left me because there was someone else who had stolen his heart. His closed off, always guarded, beautifully tortured heart. In so many ways, I was entirely shocked. I racked my wine-clouded mind: who is this person? What about this mystery girl was so unique, so utterly special that she was worth ruining our relationship, destroying five years of memories in its wake? And when would they have met? Kurt wasn't really the going-out type. More nights than not we were sinking into our aging brown leather sofa watching a TV show. Most recently, we were hooked on a tale of fire-breathing dragons and war-torn houses. He loved violent fantasy, and I loved a good downward spiral. So I was plagued by this more than anything else: how did he meet her? Who even *was* she?

~

I was deep into this sinkhole of a question when I must have finally closed my eyes and fallen asleep. The next thing I knew it was daylight, and someone was knocking on my front door. I checked my phone – 1 p.m. How the hell was it so late? I had five missed calls from Pheebs. I peeled my body off of the bed, I guess I had wound up there eventually, and drifted towards the door. Still a tad drunk, I wasn't ready for the barrage of frustration from my frantic friend.

"What the *hell*, Brett?! You can't just *not* answer your phone after you tell me something like this! I was worried the *entire* four hours I was in the car! I was worried you'd, I don't even *know*."

She still lived in the town in which we went to college. Tallahassee. She wanted to move for many reasons, but the biggest was that she was constantly reminded that all the memories in that city would never be repeated. Our entire friend group had moved away after graduation. We may have all started our lives in different places, but once every year or two, we all found ourselves back in Tallahassee and with Phoebe. It had truly given us so much, and we liked to make a pilgrimage to pay our respects whenever we were able.

"I know, I'm sorry. Listen, I just woke up. I must have fallen asleep and I guess I *really* needed it. I literally just woke up." I said between yawns.

"*Ugh*, okay. It's fine, I'm glad that you fell asleep. From the way you sounded on the phone, I didn't think you would." She was calming down, slowly but surely. Truthfully, she could get revved up over nothing. I constantly called her an angry troll.

"Yeah, me neither. There's a lot to fill you in on here, Pheebs. Come in. There's food in the fridge if you're hungry."

She dropped her bags by the door. They were adorable, very much her style. Sea foam green with yellow flowers scattered across the fabric. She was an outdoorsy girl, grew up in a small town in north Florida. But surprisingly, she landed on the girly side of things more often than not. In this respect was one of the only ways we differed. She loved vibrant clothes; I wore mostly dark colors. Her nails were always done professionally and in pastel shades. I did mine myself and typically they were black. She always gave me shit for that. She'd constantly harass me, telling me that my nails made me look like an angsty teen in the 90s trying to piss off her parents. On the rare occasion that I'd let her drag me to a nail salon, she'd force me to pick a brighter color. The lightest I ever went was a deep red.

Actually, Kurt's proposal may have been a total surprise had it not been for Pheebs. On the night before Valentine's Day, she called me to ask what Kurt had planned for the holiday. When I told her that it was just a day in the park, she asked me to send her a picture of my nails. Skeptical of why I needed to do this but realizing that Phoebe was, in fact, that weird and controlling of a friend, I told her that they were unpainted. She demanded that they be coated with the shade she had bought me the last time we'd been together, a light greyish pink.

It was in that moment that I realized Kurt was planning on proposing and that he must have been planning it with Phoebe. I didn't let her know that I had caught on and yielded to her demands. The next day, when I took pictures of my left hand adorned with Kurt's grandmother's antique ring, I realized how grateful I was to have such a bossy, type-A best friend. She had been right, my nails looked elegant with that ring.

Sandwich in hand, always ham and cheese with no toppings except mayonnaise, she sat next to me on the couch. For the next few hours, I barely took a breath. In what felt like an avalanche of words, I told her everything. How he'd left, what I'd found in his notebook, and what I wanted to do next.

"I just need to know who she is. I can't imagine how he even met her, Pheebs. Like, he doesn't go out," I said as I looked into the palms of my hands. It was all so confusing.

"I'm honestly still blown away. I just don't understand. Especially the timing – two months before the wedding. What an *asshole*."

She said the last word with such ferocity, I forgot that she was barely five-feet tall. She was not frightening in the traditional sense, but, man, piss her off and you've got a tiny ball of pure fury on your hands. There were many times in college that she came to my defense, whether it be a drunk girl at a bar who thought she saw me glancing at her man, or my ex, Stan, whom she truly did not believe was worthy of being with me. I remember one night he told me I couldn't go out with my girlfriends because he wouldn't be there. Mind you, I had never cheated on him, and he had actually been the one to cheat on me in the beginning of our relationship.

Phoebe called him up, three drinks of cheap vodka in her system, and told him to go display his toxic masculinity elsewhere—we were going out, and I would call him later. I broke up with him about a week after that. She was right, as usual, and he didn't deserve me. I heard that Stan's next girlfriend left him for a guy she met at a bar one night. What a twisted case of conjuring up your own fate.

"Maybe they work together?" I ruminated as I poured her another glass of wine.

"I guess they could have. Or maybe online? I mean, you never know what people do with their phones anymore."

"Yeah, I mean, Jesus, there are like thirty different dating apps now. You can hide that shit so easily, I'm sure," I said. But I had no idea. I had been taken since the dating apps hit the market. Oh, *God*, was that my future?

"That did happen to my friend, actually. Her husband was on some super secretive site where you find people to have affairs with. He did that shit for *years*, too. I mean, I'm not saying Kurt did that," she said, hesitantly monitoring my reaction.

"No, I get what you're saying. It just… doesn't make sense, Pheebs. That's not the Kurt that I know, right? That we know? But I guess neither is the asshole that dumped me on my birthday."

Suddenly, we heard a loud bang against the front door.

"Holy *shit,* Brett! What the *fuck* was that?!"

Phoebe sprang up from the kitchen table and dropped her glass of wine, shattering the crystal across the stone floor. The deep red spread throughout the tiles, following the lines in between each square. Another one bites the dust. I'm going to need to buy another set, I reminded myself.

"Oh, those little *fuckers,*" I said jumping up looking for a flashlight, "it's the asshole kids who live in this neighborhood, man."

I darted to the front door, unlocked the handle and swung it open with a loud thud against the side of the house. As I looked out and to my left, I heard laughing. All I saw was the slight shine of their bike's reflectors receding in the late evening nightfall.

"I knew it. It's just stupid kids. They do this all the time. Kurt and I woke up to our mailbox bashed in one morning."

"Dude, are you kidding me? Call the cops or something, that's destruction of property."

Always ready to fight. I should talk to her about that, I thought.

"I mean, we tried that once. Kurt went down to the station and reported it. Nothing happened, though. Fucking shocker."

"Well, what about your landlord? Maybe he knows the kids. I mean, he lives around the corner. Hell, they could be *his* little brats."

Phoebe had no patience for kids. She wasn't a fan of children, and often complained to me that she'd never have them. I bet her she'd change her mind by the time she was thirty. So far, she hadn't budged.

"I tried calling my landlord, but he doesn't do anything. He said it's not his problem."

"Brett, you need to get out of here, this neighborhood is *terrible*. And you have that shitty lock on your door that's not doing anything. Honestly, you should have moved a while ago. But now that… Kurt's gone, I think that you should seriously start looking at a new place to live. Somewhere safer."

Living in the ruins of my relationship was hard enough but adding in the fact that I was now living alone in a sketchy neighborhood would keep me up at night. I had let Kurt do the house shopping when we were looking years ago: I had just started my internship at the time and was swamped with work. So, I said if he could find a two-bedroom, one-bathroom home for a fair price near downtown Orlando I'd be in. I should have known what that would actually get me. We were pretty damn far from downtown, off the beaten path on Michigan Street. The neighborhood was unsettling, to say the least. A shitty Shell gas station perched eerily at the corner and a rotting pizza shop next to it. The neighbors mostly kept to themselves, but their kids didn't seem to follow their lead. Kurt and I were constantly waking up to broken beer bottles and blunt wrappers scattered across the front yard. The kids biked around at night, drinking and not giving a shit about anyone else.

Some of that is typical adolescent bullshit, and I could shrug it off as such when Kurt was living with me. However, now that the man of the house had left, I felt vulnerable. Living alone as a female is always a bit unnerving. Our Muppet-sized house was located near a small park at the lake, which was a surprisingly hopeful spot, in theory. But our little neighborhood was across from a juvenile detention center and that quaint little park was well known to be visited by heroin addicts, looking to shoot up. About a year after living there, a young woman overdosed on the park bench. Her strung-out boyfriend knocked at my door at eight a.m., asking to use my phone to call an ambulance. I was alone, but he was kind to me. Afterwards, I felt so badly for him that I gave him a beer and a joint. Kurt was not amused by that. Apparently, I was too trusting. "That will bite you on the ass one day, Brett," he told me.

~

Phoebe and I spent a few more hours talking about what a fucked-up situation I was in. I hadn't even taken a pause to consider the most immediate concern: the wedding. It finally donned on me that I had the most painful task yet ahead of me. I had to contact everyone on the guest list and inform them that the most beautiful day of my life, the event that everyone who loved me could not wait to attend, was cancelled due to a runaway groom. How many long-winded phone calls with extended relatives did I have to endure? All the times I would soon hear "I'm so sorry" and "you don't realize it now, but, this is the best thing that could happen to you" or "at least you didn't have kids" and even "God, could you imagine if you had to go through a *divorce*?" Even thinking about it made me want to scream into a pillow.

"Honestly, what blows my mind was that I somehow didn't see it coming, Phoebe. I mean how fucking *stupid* am I?" I said after finishing my glass and, as it turned out, the rest of our bottle of wine.

"Nope, we're not doing that. Don't even start to blame yourself. This is *not* your fault! None of us could have seen this coming. I mean, you two were end game. You were together for so long, and the wedding was so soon. No one is going to think "damn, she really should have known.""

"Well, sure, okay, not in the most obvious way. But, Pheebs, it was the stuff that was happening that I never picked up on. Remember how many times I would call you bitching that he wasn't helping with the wedding planning? I mean, really, he didn't even want to help pick out the color theme. He never visited the venue. That was a sign, I just wasn't picking up what he was putting down."

I'd just used his phrase.
Another little knife in the heart.

"I mean, sure. But, you know, I just assumed he was a guy and wasn't really into the whole 'wedding planning' process. I mean, he wasn't exactly interested in those things. Really, I don't think you should have known from something like that."

"No, man. It was all there—plain as day. Why the hell didn't I stop for a second and ask him, is this just boring to you, or is this maybe not what you want?"

Hindsight.
Useless.

"Because, Brett, when did he ever talk to you about anything?"

And she was right. Therein lay our biggest problem, our largest obstacle that we chose to live with instead of conquer. To ignore instead of extinguish. We lacked communication. Truthful conversation, sometimes painfully so. But also curative for fixing any broken stones met along the path. We lacked that honest communication that is the backbone to any healthy and durable relationship. The kind that can turn a mountain into a molehill. But Kurt and I never talked about our feelings, because he never really let me in. He only ever let me peek behind his firm, unyielding walls and, slowly but surely, he sealed me out of even that elusive gift. I learned more about him by reading his notebook for five minutes than I learned through spending five years by his side.

"Alright, I think it's time to call my parents," I said. I was unprepared for the weight of that task.

"*Dude,* you haven't told them what happened yet?! Oh, man, Brett. They're going to be heartbroken. Your mom has been texting me about your rehearsal dinner for months," Phoebe said, not realizing how much harder it was for me to feel my parents' heartbreak than my own.

"Shit. Yeah, this is going to be rough. I really could use a sibling to take the heat off of me for a bit through this. Walt and Terry are going to helicopter parent *hard* for a while after I tell them."

I was my parents' only child, but not because I was a mistake or because they didn't want more kids. My parents, Walt and Terry, met decently late in life. Each engulfed in unhappy marriages for most of their prime years, they finally divorced their useless other halves and within a year, they found one another. According to my father, he was a bit of a playboy most of his life. A job as a wealthy lawyer with a reputation for falling for beautiful women will do that to a man. But he told me constantly that when he saw my mother walk into the room on their first date, it was game-over. He was in love, and he wanted to give this woman the world. Terry was smart, a real-estate agent with a knack for being both kind and assertive, and she could make him laugh. Really, she could entertain anyone for days on end, including herself. She told me once that her favourite compliment she'd ever received was from an ex-boyfriend in her high school yearbook. It said, "Put Terry in a room by herself, and she'll be entertained for hours." I adored that about her.

Within a year they were married. And like clockwork, with no time wasted, I was born less than a year later. They were natural parents: they loved having a child more than I think anyone in history ever has. I was showered with so much affection. I know this from the countless home videos they recorded of me doing just about anything at all. In every video, what I was doing was entirely pointless. In one, I am merely sitting on my tiny-person sofa in just a diaper, watching TV while surrounded by every single one of my stuffed animals in concentric circles. Truly humiliating to re-watch as an adult. What made that tape irreplaceable to me was what I heard in the background: my parents talking to one another, saying how much they loved me and how they couldn't imagine their lives had they not met and had a child together. Part of me thinks this is the moment they realized they wanted to have another baby.

And then for a little while, the home videos included my little brother in the form of a baby bump. My mother was pregnant a second time at forty-four years old. I was just two at the time, so I can't recall anything about this period of our family's history. I don't even remember the night that my mom came home from the hospital with no bump and no baby. My little brother, Morris, had died just a moment after he had been born into this world and had taken his very first breath. Morris had lived an entire life in just seconds. My parents were devastated, Morris was buried at the cemetery in a plot the size of a small stack of books, and his death was something we never really mentioned as a family again. Some nights, when my mom had a few glasses of wine, she'd ask me what I thought Morris might have looked like. I never let myself think about that, I told her. It was almost more painful to wonder about him had he lived than to just pretend he never existed at all. It wasn't the perfect coping mechanism, but it worked for me.

Phoebe opened up the second bottle of wine that she pulled out of her bag Mary Poppins style, and poured me another glass. I picked up my phone and dialed my mother's cell.

"Hi, honey! How is your first full day of being twenty-six?" she asked lightly.

I could feel her warm smile through the phone. I held back tears with all the strength I could muster. The wine had made the dam start to loosen up once again and I could feel them pooling.

All I wanted to do was collapse into myself. I felt the tears settle into the corners of my eyes, but I stopped before I could start. The wise words of my grandmother, Ann, were echoing in my mind. "Whenever I feel like crying, Brett, I take a moment and I swallow instead. It all just goes away." I swallowed, and the feeling passed. I thought about what my grandmother would say to me now. What kind of sage advice could she offer me?

She had lived with us since I was an annoying middle schooler hell-bent on destroying everything in my path. Where my parents failed to discipline me, she picked up the slack. They weren't home enough to see that I was heading for the danger zone. Totally untamable. I remember one evening, on one particularly hormonally driven rampage, I told her that I hated her. All four-foot-eleven-inches of her straightening, she looked me in the eyes, arms bent at her hips, and she roared, "Yeah, well, I hate you, too!" Nothing could have been further from the truth for either of us. I was her only grandchild, and we adored each other. But in that moment, I needed to hear it. I needed a wake-up call. And she was happy to be the one to dial the phone.

That woman was one of the most incredible human beings this world has ever seen. She was a force to be reckoned with. And I was lucky enough to call her my grandmother. She was also my very best friend. She had only passed a few years ago, but it still hurt me like a fresh wound. Every time I walked into my parent's home and she wasn't waiting on the couch by the front door ready to greet me, I felt the salt sprinkle. God, I missed her with every part of my soul.

"Hey, mom. So... uh, I have some...news. I really *really* don't want to get into it right now, but Kurt broke up with me. The wedding's off and

I need your help. How exactly do you cancel an entire wedding?" I asked while trying to remain focused on the task at hand. All facts, no feelings.

"Oh, no, *sweetheart*... What happened? Are you okay? Oh, I know you don't want to talk about it. I am just... I don't even know what to say," she whispered. All I wanted was to be wrapped in her arms.

"Yeah, I'm okay, mom. Phoebe's here. I just... I don't know where to start with canceling everything. Do I tell guests first? Do you have the number for the venue? I mean, seriously, what the *fuck* do I do now?"

I knew she didn't love when I used that word. But I was too tired to edit myself.

"Okay, don't worry about that, Brett. Your father and I will take care of that. Just be with Phoebe and give her a hug and a 'thank you' from us for being there when you needed her. When you're ready to talk, your dad and I are here, okay?"

"Thanks mom. I love you."

"We love you too, honey. You dad says you may not be ready for a joke yet, but he wants to let you know that you're better off without Kurt. He was lousy with a deck of cards and couldn't play euchre for shit."

My dad wasn't great at sentimental moments, but he could always make the heavy moments feel a bit lighter. And, boy, did he love me.

"Yeah, what a loser," I said without letting on how much I was really hurting.

And with that last jab at Kurt's character from my father, our call ended.

~

The next few days were a blur of sympathetic phone calls from friends and family and compassionate emails from wedding vendors who had just lost our business but wished me the best in this "trying time." In truth, I remembered almost nothing of the few days after the breakup. I'm sure the days called off from work and multitude of wine corks garnishing my tile floors had a lot to do with that. But honestly, it was as if the same was true of devastating moments as it was of the happy ones. The mind wipes the slate clean. Tabula Rasa. And I was too busy trying to escape my new reality to focus on the aching moments passing me by.

If it weren't for Phoebe's presence, I'm not sure that I would have even fed myself. I was barely able to do that anyway. I desired nothing; my stomach was continuously unsettled. It was like that feeling you get before you do something that you're nervous for. It never went away. I just couldn't bring myself to eat. Even weed couldn't fix that and, trust me, Phoebe and I tried it.

The days continuously floated by and Phoebe stayed with me. She barely left my side. The only time she ever took her attention away from me was to answer her phone. She had been receiving texts from her boyfriend, Seth, often. His dad had recently died from cancer, myeloma, and it was truly brutal. Violent and ferocious. After years of experimental drugs and excruciating bone marrow transplants it had killed him and torn his family apart from the roots. Seth was his only son and Phoebe told me how much his father's loss had devastated him. She had to make sure she answered him whenever he needed her, but it was wearing her down. I could see it in her eyes when she'd get a text from him. She'd get this look on her face, almost guilty. Like she felt bad for enjoying herself while Seth was falling apart in their apartment back in Tallahassee. After one such text when I caught her expression spread across her face, I asked her about it.

"Pheebs, you okay? You look stressed."

"What? Oh, sorry," she said closing her phone. "Uh, yeah, Seth is just having a rough night tonight."

"Anything I can do to help? I feel bad keeping you here." Was I being too selfish?

"Oh, my God, no. You need me. I know he does, too, but he can always go see his friends in his band. They're performing at King's this weekend, you know."

A change in subject. That's okay, she didn't want to talk about it.

"Oh, *shit!* I remember that bar! God, remember that one night that we all ended up walking home at, like, four a.m.? We were *so* drunk! You were leaning on me, and Kurt—"

I stopped speaking after saying his name.
Kurt.

It had become this looming presence, like I was afraid I'd summon him if I kept talking. But wouldn't I want that?

"Well, anyways, Seth will send us some videos. The place looks the same, you know," Phoebe said, trying to ease the tension.

"Yeah, sounds good. Always nice to reminisce."

But it wasn't, because all of my memories were tainted, now.

CHAPTER 5

After about a week of joining me in destructive behavior labeled self-care, Phoebe went home. She still had a job, a life and a boyfriend that needed her, and she couldn't keep day drinking with me without losing the first on that list. Before she left, she spent a few nights with me downing dollar beers at many of the local dive bars downtown. Downtown Orlando was a typical city blend of wannabe high rollers who spent too much money on nice clothes and women, and college students with bad fakes who relied on the aforementioned type of people to get hammered.

I had gone downtown with Kurt only a few times over the years. Just a handful, maybe. Usually I had to drag him out, as the four corners of our house were always more appealing somehow. In fact, New Year's Eve a few years ago was nearly spent there, surrounded by those walls. It was about 10 o'clock, and we were in the full swing of mismatched pajamas and freshly packed bowls of weed. Kurt and I had discussed doing something, just us, to ring in the New Year. He said it would save us the hassle of stifling crowds and jacked-up alcohol pricing. I still would have liked to go out with friends, but he didn't exactly enjoy their company.

I had about four girl friends who still lived in Orlando that I knew from high school. We'd grown up together, endured the truly painful years of our conservative Catholic schooling together, and hadn't lost touch since senior year. They were all originally meant to be bridesmaids in my wedding, actually. I guess all that time together had allowed me to overlook how truly toxic our friendships had become over the years. Old grudges and all that. I stopped talking to them about towards the end of Kurt's and my engagement.

The last New Year's Eve Kurt and I were together, I received a heated text from the most poisonous of those girls. Kathy. She always seemed to deliver a truly unique blend of harsh judgement mixed with condescending and totally misguided elitism. Her extreme height allowed her to rule over all five-feet of me with ease. God, and that *laugh* she had. I never got used to it. Loud, obnoxious. She always needed attention wherever she went, and she usually got it by being the noisiest in the room with the most to say. I was always apologizing for her when we met new people. That New Year's, she commanded me to join her downtown. She was with the other friends of ours, and they refused to accept my and Kurt's "lay low" evening.

"So, Kathy says she and the girls are out tonight and have a table at Mandy's. I know you love how full they pour those shots," I said, nudging Kurt playfully.

He loved a nice, tall shot of Jameson, and this bar seemed to think that filling a beer glass half-way constituted merely a stiff pour. It was the most fun I'd had in town while securing the most damage.

"Oh, *Brett*, c'mon. You know how I feel about them. Your high school friends suck, babe. They're so mean to you, and you just... take it. It's hard to watch. It's like a scene from *Mean Girls*," he said. I'd recently convinced him to watch that. I would have been proud of this reference had I not been so frustrated with his attitude.

"Babe, *please*, it's New Year's! C'mon, I want to ring in 2015 in a dress." I pulled my shirt down, playfully. After a few years together, I knew what made him tick.

"Okay, okay. Fine."

He furrowed his brow and looked my way. I still remember how he would look at me in moments like these. Part intrigue, part frustration.

Like he wasn't ever totally sure of what I would come up with next. Yes, the impulsiveness I possessed in my early twenties was tiresome. But I never missed the look on his face once he given in to my demands. He liked this about me. Well, I thought he did. He then rolled his eyes and burrowed his face into my cleavage. Time stopped after that. Needless to say, Kathy wasn't impressed with how much time it took us to bring ourselves to leave the bed and actually make it to the bar.

I had to twist his arm, but it was going to be worth it, I told myself. We'd enjoy ourselves. Start going out more. I couldn't have been more wrong. The night was a disaster, and I was left regretting leaving that sunken, brown, tired, leather couch. Kurt was pulled into some high school drama between us all and the night ended in tears. That was one of the last nights we all spoke. I don't think Kurt and I went out again after that. Honestly, I couldn't blame him. As much as it hurt me to lose those girls at first, I was thankful eventually. Sure, it was lonely here. They were the only friends I had within hours. But Kurt had been right, they weren't good friends. I never told him how right he was about them. I wish I could now.

~

Shitty memory aside, I was excited to be out again. And I had my best friend with me. Phoebe and I had always been partiers when we were single together in college. After the first few outings since the breakup, I realized how much I had actually kind of missed that lifestyle. In a lot of ways, getting into a serious relationship in my early twenties had deprived me of those wild, selfish, growing years. The years when your only responsibilities were school and a minimum wage job that allowed for you to still cultivate a healthy social life. I never really had a one-night stand, either. Well, no night that ended with one-time sex, anyways. I was always the type of person who caught feelings for anyone I had slept with. I constantly tried to mold a misguided relationship from any source of pretend affection.

On the Saturday night before Phoebe was leaving to go back home, we wound up at a local downtown Orlando hotspot, Moondance. It was the perfect mix of dive bar and dance club, serving cheap drinks and truly embarrassing, tequila-inspired dance moves. Walking inside of the bar, I was met with twirling strobe lights, pirouetting across the walls and floor. The floor was sticky, a little decrepit. There was a sour smell. A life-sized Captain Morgan statue, fully decorated, sat in the corner.

This was my second night there in a row and my first night trying to find someone to take home. Sure, it was maybe a little too soon to find someone to spend the night having sloppy, drunken sex with, but I was over feeling sorry for myself. I still hadn't heard from Kurt. Well, except for him telling me that he was stopping by one evening to pick up some of his things when I was out. You know, so as not to make this "any harder than it already is." Did he remember his dishes? I know they were his mothers.

Kurt.

In truth, I spent most of the first night searching for him in the crowd. I don't know why I thought he'd be there. I wanted to find him with the woman he wrote about. I wanted to see who it was that inspired such lyricism. It was more painful to me that this woman could arouse the emotional expression in those ballads than it was that she could make him leave me. The way she inspired him to open up. All that emotion. But my search proved useless and I wasn't wasting another night. I was pissed, I wanted a rebound, and I was determined to find one.

As Phoebe and I were sharing a couple of vodka sodas, we heard voices shouting from the corner of the bar. Drawn to the commotion, we walked over to a big crowd of people who all seemed to be enjoying the hell out of their nights. They were circled around a huge wooden table covered with dozens of little red plastic cups. Phoebe nudged me and pointed out a group of three people, two guys and a girl. My eyes locked on one in particular.

He was the epitome of tall, dark and handsome. I was new to flirting after years of being out of practice and Phoebe took the opportunity to walk up to him. She was always so fearless. As she marched over with purpose, I followed timidly. I struggled to catch my breath. They were all laughing together, but he was all I could hear. His laugh was so lively, so uninhibited that it made me smile quietly to myself. He carried himself so...freely, I thought. I'd missed being around that type of lightness. With such a strong energy, he drew me in instantly, and I was a moth to his flame. I told myself I had done it. Mission accomplished. I wanted him. Badly.

"Hey! What are ya'll playing?" Phoebe asked while leaning over the table in front of the handsome stranger, strategically showing off her cleavage for the men across from the table to ogle. She actually distracted one such gentleman so well that he missed his turn and was swiftly engulfed in a chant to "Drink! Drink! Drink!" his beer.

"Well, *hey* there. It's called Chandelier. Watch a round, it's easy to pick up. What's your name? I'm Luke." He smiled. I was stupefied.

"I'm Phoebe. This is my best friend, Brett. She's really good at drinking games, actually. Do you need a partner?" She was the best wing-woman. I needed to buy her a drink for that one.

"Nice to meet you both. Actually, we could use a few pretty girls on our team. Brett, do you like drinking really shitty beer, really quickly?" He was so dreamy, I got lost in his light brown eyes and my own tipsy stupor for a moment.

"I mean, if it has a percentage, hand it over!" In my mind this was a clever response, but it sounded stupid after it left my lips. Confidence, Brett.

"Well, *alllllllright*! I like a lady who knows how to drink. Stand next to me, lets fuck over Tom. He looks thirsty."

By that way he nudged the guy next to him, I presumed Tom was his friend to his left. Not the most handsome guy in the world but he had a really kind smile. The kind that lit up a room with its warmth. The type that you could instantly trust.

"Yeah, okay, fuck off, Luke. Hey, nice to meet you, Brett! I'm Tom and this hottie next to me is my paid girlfriend. No one would be dumb enough to date me free of charge," he said. Ah, the showboater of the group.

The girl next to him rolled her eyes and gave me a wave. She was beautiful. Tall, blonde, athletic. Her outfit perfectly matched and her jewelry sparkled. I noticed her bag was monogrammed. She was so put together. It was almost eerie. But her smile was warm, and I oddly really wanted her to like me.

"Yeah, clearly I don't know how to pick 'em. I'm Lana! So nice to meet you! Now let's play some fucking *chandelierrrrr!*"

And with that roar, the table went wild. Fists pounding, cups flipping, people chugging. It was exhilarating. It was the most I'd smiled since my birthday, and the most alive I'd felt in years. With each round we played, I felt myself become lighter. With each drink I threw back, I moved further from the timid girl who entered the bar that night and a step closer to a more self-assured version of myself.

I remembered now how I gained my confidence in college: lots of cheap beer and a lack of thinking. I was typically so drunk that I was constantly drowning that little voice in my head that said I shouldn't do whatever it was I was doing. A few mistakes were made that way. I had once challenged an old boyfriend to a race back to his apartment. I jumped the railing outside his door and landed on my shoulder, dislocating it and suffering some pretty bad cement-burn on my skin. But I had also made some of my best decisions after throwing back arguably a few too many.

The first time I'd grown the courage to kiss Kurt was after many rounds of beer pong at a friend's house. I had turned to him, we locked eyes, and then my lips were against his. It was one of those first kisses that you feel everywhere. I knew it was the start of something significant. Afterward, we'd spent a sweet and intimate night beneath his tie-dyed tapestry. Every time he touched me, it sent sparks throughout my bare skin. The thought of Kurt sent my stomach up to my throat.

Kurt.

Now that I was here, could I still say that that was one of my best decisions? Or should I call it a mistake? I pulled myself by the ears out of that rabbit hole before I could go too far down into it. I wasn't performing as Alice today.

We played chandelier for about an hour before Luke and I moved towards the bar. Phoebe had tactically pulled herself away from us after the game had ended and was in the middle of a conversation with Lana and Tom. I felt Luke staring at me as I waited for my vodka soda with a sliver of lime. I was so nervous that I ignored him. I couldn't bring myself to meet his gaze. I laid my forearms against the sticky, marbled counter and tried to breathe. My heart was skipping. Finally, we got our drinks and I followed him over to the rest of our small group.

"So, what's the topic over here?" I asked none of them in particular. I was still too anxious to spend time alone with Luke. Tom smiled as we approached.

"Well, Phoebe over here, is telling us some seriously *amazing* tales of your shenanigans in college, Brett," Tom said, smirking.

"Oh, *is* she?" I asked turning my stare questioningly her way.

Phoebe looked at me with a devious smile. "Well, I mean, just the good ones. Like when you woke up the morning after a party with a cream cheese bagel stuck to your face."

Tom and Lana were laughing hysterically. Luke looked at me curiously, a massive smile spreading across his face. God, how I wanted to kiss him in that moment.

"Wow, Pheebs. Thanks for that," I giggled, blushing. "To be fair, you were the one mixing those drinks. It's your fault."

"Sure, but I didn't tell you to chug them! That was all you, lady," she said, lightly shoving me.

"I love that," Luke said to me. "You were just prepared for the hang-over the next morning. Being proactive and making yourself breakfast. I can learn a lot from you, I think. Pheebs," he said as he turned toward her while putting his arm around my waist, "I need to hear more stories about this wild child I got here."

My entire body felt this slight movement. His fingertips slowly traced the small of my back as he moved his hands from one side of my body to the other. I wanted more.

"Hey, Pheebs, let's go play another round. I'm just warming up," I said, moving my hand to meet Luke's on my waist.

"Uh, yeah, just give me second. I need to answer this. It's Seth."

He was texting her all night. This was the first time she stopped to answer. I felt bad for her. It was a lot for her to handle, and things for Seth weren't seeming to get any easier. But I understood. He was going through something excruciating, and she loved him. They had been together as long as Kurt and I.

Kurt.
No.

"Ooh, the *boyfriend*, huh? Tell him to let you *live*, man! Or at least come down here and party with us, shit!" Tom was hammered and clearly didn't know what was going on with Seth and his family.

"Uh, yeah, the *boyfriend*," she said playfully.

She wasn't one to bring down the mood, but I could tell she was frazzled. A bit overwhelmed by whatever it was he had texted her. She quickly answered it and slid her phone into her purse. Pink. Kate Spade. *So* Phoebe.

"Alright, let's get it!" Lana pulled her to the table.

Tom followed, teetering a bit as he walked. He placed a hand on her lower back, slowly moving down to her skirt. He was too big to be swaying. Muscles must not come easy to him, I thought, but he was a naturally strong guy. In that moment, I was happy he seemed to be such a gentle giant.

Luke pulled me with him as we followed the rest of the crew. It felt like I belonged.

~

Finally, 2 a.m. rolled around and we were given the telltale sign: flashing lights on and off, all around Moondance. The crowds were dispersing. It was time to go home. Phoebe and I walked out of the bar with the same energetic crew and I said goodnight to the strangers I'd met in passing that night. Luke turned towards me and put his arm around my shoulders.

"Yeah, so we're planning on hitting up this new club next weekend. You two should come by on Friday. We usually pregame at Tom and Lana's place," Luke said, his hand playing with the hair in my ponytail. I couldn't help but imagine those strong fingers tracing my bare skin.

"Well, Phoebe doesn't live here and has to go home, unfortunately, but I would definitely be down. If there's drinking involved, I'm there," I said, sliding my finger into his belt loop.

I wondered if I was doing this right. Is this how you flirt? Luke curled his pointer finger under my chin, lifted up my face, lowered his head and brought his eyes to meet my gaze. Softly, he kissed me. It was only a second. Quick, sweet. I melted into him.

"Alright, trouble. I'd better see you there." He peeled himself away and took a step back. Smoothly, he turned and caught up with Tom and Lana.

"I'll text you the details, Brett," Lana shouted back to me, "See you next Friday! Nice to meet you both."

Phoebe and I waved goodbye to our new friends and quickly shoveled ourselves into the Uber we had called to take us home. I waited until the door was closed to betray the cool, calm and collected exterior I had tried to maintain after being kissed by what felt like my own personal Greek god.

"Holy SHIT, Brett! He was *so* incredibly *hot*! I am so proud of you right now, I'm going to order us a pizza. *Whatever* you want, man, you deserve it. I mean, did you *see* him?! Oh, dude, how was that kiss? *Please*, tell me! Let me live vicariously through you," Phoebe demanded. She was hammered, and her mouth was moving at warp speed. I was still in a daze and couldn't keep up.

"Dude… that was fucking *fireworks*. Like, the shit you dream about. I felt like I was in a movie. I'm just pissed he didn't offer to come home with me. Is it weird that he didn't?"

"No, he *totally* wanted to! He probably didn't want to make you have to leave me behind. So, if you think about it, he's hot as hell *and* he is a decent guy. Like, marry him already," she blurted out and instantly turned pale.

She knew she had said something stupid. In that moment, all the happiness I felt, all that opportunity I was craving had vanished. It had come and gone; swiftly, like the skyscrapers that passed by the car window. Now, in that moment, all I wanted was to come home to Kurt.

Kurt.

I rubbed the area on my left finger where my engagement ring should still have been. Who was she? I tried to pull myself together.

"Oh, Pheebs, you're fine. He's not on my mind at all. Trust me." Lies. "I'll make sure to let you know what happens on Friday. With any luck, I'll have *plenty* to tell," I said while trying to hide the pain in my voice.

Who was she?

Looking out the taxi window, I suddenly felt the high I'd been riding all night crash. resentfully. What was I thinking? Who gave a shit about this Luke guy, anyways? There was no way he actually cared about me. He hadn't even asked anything about me the entire night. I was just the fresh catch of the evening. The pathetic girl at the bar, longing for attention. I was completely senseless for allowing myself to feel like I mattered to him. With one achingly good kiss, I opened my heart. Maybe it was only the size of a slivered moon, like a clam shell quietly unlocking itself just enough to allow in a gust of the ocean, but quickly shutting itself off again to any possible danger.

But why would I consider opening my heart again so soon? Hell, why consider doing it ever again. He'd probably just end up breaking it in the end and leave me with the tiny, insignificant pieces, like grains of sand swiftly sifting between my fingertips. I wouldn't risk it, falling on my hands and knees attempting to collect myself again. The pain of slicing my own skin on the many shards of broken pieces that surrounded me. The idea sent a feeling of nausea throughout my entire body. All I wanted was to turn back time and comb through my past for the moment that I lost Kurt.

Kurt.

CHAPTER 6

An entirely uneventful and yet somehow completely exhausting couple of days had passed. After Phoebe left to drive four hours north to her house in our old college town, I felt like I was detoxing. I was coming down from the high of my exciting reintroduction to singledom, and now this painful realization slowly crept into my mind: I was alone, and this was the new normal. It was sharply sobering, and it poisoned my days.

As I sat at home watching T.V. on Wednesday night, I fumbled with my notes from the meeting we'd had at work earlier that day. Fuck, I'd really dropped the ball at my job. Waking up early from nights of restless sleep and spending my days at my nine-to-five depleted me of any hope I had that I would keep my life together post-breakup. I couldn't focus on my tasks. Even just grabbing coffee for my boss, Cheryl, felt like running sprints up a steep, dirt ridden hill with a boulder on my back. Every time I thought I was moving forward, I was pummeled back down ten, twenty feet. A slight step I took in the right direction felt useless; I could only feel the bottom of the hill pulling me back down.

I couldn't stop imagining Kurt holding on to the girl in his poem. Loving her, kissing her. Breathing verses into her ear. Sharing himself with her. I was never able to give her a face in my mind, but I knew it had to be faultless. The picture-perfect image of a woman who inspired sonnets. Like

Helen of Troy, her beauty sending ships across the ocean. I would catch my reflection in the black mirror of my sleeping computer. There was nothing special in that image. I was nothing special.

As I tried my best to focus on work that Wednesday night, I caught myself staring into the dark screen of my T.V. That same, unremarkable face was looking at me yet again. It mocked me. It told me that I wasn't good enough. Not marriage material. Loveless. Useless. I threw my notebook at the screen.

"Jesus, Brett, pull yourself together," I said to myself as I walked over to the T.V. to retrieve my notebook. I was frustrated. I knew that I was spiraling, but I couldn't bring myself to stop. I just didn't care enough.

The moment I sat back down on the bed, I heard a branch break. It was a loud "crack." It sounded like it came from right outside my front door. Oh great, I thought, just what I need. The neighborhood kids are on the move, yet again. I knew that they liked to bike around at night, drinking stolen beers from their inattentive parents. But this wasn't rebellious youth passing by my house. Those idiots were there, lurking on my property. They were fucking with me, now. I went up to the window next, opened the curtain, and looked out into the pitch-black darkness. Nothing. As I closed the door and locked my tiny handle, I heard leaves rustling and branches snapping. The sound was quieter as it continued. Footsteps leaving? I opened the door.

"Whoever is out there," I yelled, "I called the police and they're on their way!"

I lied about calling the cops, but I knew that if I heard the sound again, I would call them. But, ten minutes passed, and I heard nothing. Just the wind and my racing thoughts. But I thought it was better to be safe than sorry and I typed in Kurt's number. We hadn't spoken since he left, and he was probably off with his new muse. The woman who inspired him to write such beautiful poetry. I felt a mixture of sadness and betrayal. I soaked in it. I considered what I was about to do. I can't go running to my ex who deserted me because I hear things going bump in the night. How embarrassing would that be, to play the part of the damsel in distress to a man who no longer wanted to be a character in the story. After five minutes of silence, I realized that I had spun an impressive amount of panic from my isolation.

My heart was racing.
I felt like my chest wouldn't let it enough air.
Am I suffocating?

I spent the next few minutes trying to slow my breathing. It was strange. It wasn't something I'd experienced before. Opening the door to check outside a few more times, I realized there was no one there. I was alone. I wasn't being haunted by anybody but Kurt. I spent the rest of the night reading from his paper world. I wondered when I would be able to give up the ghost. My ghost. But who was she?

~

I woke up the next morning still a bit shaken. Logically, I knew that there was no one outside of my house last night, that it was all in my head. Still, as a single woman living alone in an area that could easily be deemed a location on the "bad side" of town, I needed security. I called my landlord and asked him to come put a dead-bolt lock on my door. He showed up about ten minutes after I called. When he arrived, I remembered why we never called him.

Garett was entirely undelightful, to put it kindly. He lived a few houses down and was constantly driving around the neighborhood with a gun in the waistband of his pants, monitoring his properties. He deemed himself the sheriff of our shitty little community. We mocked him and called him Batman.

"So, what do you need? I'm not fixing the washer. That's your deal." Lovely.

"*Hi,* Garett. Yeah, it's actually not about that," I said, realizing that the washer was, in fact, something I did need fixed. "I thought I heard someone outside my house last night. It was late, and I was just wondering if you could put a dead-bolt on the door." I noticed him move his hand instinctively over to his gun.

"Kurt's gone, huh?" I wondered how he knew.

"Um… yeah. We broke up and that's kind of why I need your help." I suddenly felt extremely uncomfortable to have him inside of my house.

"Well, I can do it for you. But I need to come back in about an hour. One of the goats is sick and my wife can't do anything. Fuckin' lazy since the baby." Truly charming.

Yes, the man had goats. Actually, he had an entire farm at his corner lot. His wife didn't work, but her job was a full-time one. She was never without a baby in her arms. They had five kids who ran around like beasts, shoeless. The wild things on the street. Then they had *actual* animals. Goats, peacocks, chickens, litters of German shepherds, even giant tortoises. One day he accidentally ran over one of the turtles. It was fifty years old. The entire neighborhood came out to pay our respects to this majestic creature. A makeshift funeral attended by some truly noteworthy human specimens. Garett put it out of its misery with one bullet to the head.

"Okay, um, thank you. Did you want me to be here for it?" I asked.

"Nope, got a key. I'll let myself in," he spit out as he jingled his key-ring in my face. It must have had twenty keys on it. The home was his property and he made sure that all who rented from him remembered that.

I didn't want to spend any more time with Garett than I needed to. I went out for a few hours, grabbed a coffee, and tried to get some work done. The most recent assignment was a novel written by a recently divorced man who wanted to put his marriage into the context of a horror story. All my boss wanted me to do was contact him and let him know that we wouldn't be moving forward with his book. I couldn't even type the email.

I began calling into work and informing Cheryl that I was sick. I'd been doing that a lot lately. She didn't put up too much fuss. I'd be entirely reliable until recently. I may not have been ill in the traditional sense; I had no heightened temperature to report or doctor's note to file. But every morning when I woke up and was confronted with my new reality, I became physically ill. I couldn't eat – the idea of food still made my stomach turn. I couldn't focus – my thoughts were a muddled mess with no clear path. And I definitely couldn't sleep – my mind was plagued by regret and a burning desire to turn back time.

Kurt.
Who was she?

The only curative that kept me feeling even the slightest bit myself was lighting up one of the many joints I had in my arsenal. Not working consistently had left me with plenty of time to hone my joint rolling skills and I began to consider myself an expert. I was home a lot. The weed helped me sleep but it didn't seem to affect my appetite. My body was quickly being run down to the bone and I was losing weight rapidly. By the time that next Friday rolled around, I was fitting into my favorite jeans with more of a give than I was used to. I decided that this could actually be one benefit to heartbreak. I strapped on my wedges, took a couple shots of whisky, and headed for the door. My Uber was out front, and I wanted to get to the pregame. I wanted to get to Luke.

~

As the Uber was pulling up, I texted Lana to let her know that I was outside of her and Tom's apartment. She sent me a quick text with a thumbs up and code for the elevator. I entered the complex, pressed the numbers in the lobby, and was quickly shot up to the thirteenth floor of one of the tallest buildings downtown. The elevator was entirely made of windows and revealed a breathtaking view of the city. How did they afford this place?

For a moment, I looked out at all the buildings and wondered: where is Kurt now? Is he thinking about me? Or is he with her—the anonymous girl who inspired him to write the words I wished were about me? I shook it off, now wasn't the time. Fuck them both. And fuck me for still obsessing over it all.

I walked up to their door and knocked. Tom answered the door and pulled me in for a bear hug.

"Hey, Brett! I'm so happy you could make it! Come on in, we're playing 'Never Have I Ever'. Can I make you a drink?" What a warm human. I felt naturally protected in his presence.

"Hey, Tom! Yeah, so I'm actually in a bit of a shot mood lately. Do you have any whiskey?"

"*Damn*, alright then! My kind of girl. Whiskey, coming right up. Go have a seat next to Lana. I think we're starting a new round."

I saw Lana and she stood up to engulf me in her arms. These people are all so nice, I thought. Why didn't I meet them years ago?

"Heyyyyy, babe! So good to see you again! Here, come sit between Luke and me," she gave me an entirely indiscreet wink at that suggestion. I turned bright red—the color of the plastic cups on the table—but was happy to comply. Luke turned to meet my smile.

"Well look who's here. The hot-shot publisher," he said. I guess he misunderstood what I did for a living, but I wasn't going to correct him. I just wanted to impress him.

"Yeah, yeah, yeah. What are we playing?" I asked while giving him a little nudge in the ribs with my shoulder. He patted my upper thigh. Oh boy, I thought. Keep your cool, Brett.

"It's called 'Never Have I Ever' and I think it's your turn, Brett," Lana said as Tom laughed and put his arm around her waist. We all raised our right had with three fingers extended.

"Okay, never have I ever stolen food from a grocery store," I said.

"Boo!" Tom reprimanded, "that is *so* freaking boring, Brett."

"What can I say," I said, "I'm an upstanding citizen."

"Alright, well I'm not," Tom stated, "Never have I ever done three lines of cocaine in thirty seconds."

"You fucking *liar*! You just did that five minutes ago!" Lana said, shoving him playfully. I noticed she was sniffling.

"No, that was you! I only did two," he said as he winked at me.

"Oh, well then you're not wrong," she said in between giggles. "Okay, my turn. Truth or dare."

"Lana, that's not even the game we're playing," Luke said, smiling at me and shaking his head. I guess I hadn't pre-gamed as hard as they had. I wasn't keeping up with their energy and was feeling wildly unsure of myself.

"Well, I'm changing vibes. Okay, truth or dare for... Brett!" Lana said, pointing a perfectly manicured finger my way.

"Um, okay... dare?" I said. Why not show I can party, too?

"*Awesome*, I dare you to lick a bump off of Luke's lower lip." she demanded. She seemed very pleased with herself. Tom wasn't smiling.

"Uh, Lana, maybe not the best idea. Brett, have you ever even done coke before?" he looked uncomfortable, like a brother with a watchful eye. How nice, I thought.

"I mean, not since college. But I'm down if you are." I took a shot of whiskey and stole a glance Luke's way.

"There's my little hell-raiser. Lana, hand it over."

Luke had called me *his*. I was feeling a bit drunk; my head was swimming in liquor filled waters. But Luke clearly liked this wild-side version of me. I wasn't going to lose his favour. And all I wanted in that moment was to once again feel my lips on his. Warm, soft. Lana handed him the tiny plastic bag. He poured some of the snow-white powder out onto the clean, glass table and licked his lips. He took a pinch of the powder and he placed it delicately upon his lower lip. I watched him complete this casual act as if he were painting the Mona Lisa. The end result was just as magnificent. Slowly, I leaned my body towards him and with my mouth an inch away from his, I felt the slightest breath escaping from the parting of his lips. Hot and intoxicating. I kissed him; the taste a virulent blend of whiskey and cocaine. Within seconds, I felt a surge of wild energy. I didn't know what I wanted more of in that moment: the blow, or Luke. We were still looking into each other's eyes when I heard Tom clear his throat.

"Um, maybe we should end the pregame here. Let's head to the club. I think some of my friends are waiting for us, anyways." Tom sounded uncomfortable.

"Ugh, fine. But first round is on you," Lana declared, pulling him up from the couch.

"Coming, trouble?" Luke asked, standing. He offered me his hand.

"Maybe, what's in it for me?" I asked.

Luke grabbed my wrist and hauled me up to stand in front of him. He was at least six-feet tall, and all five-feet of me didn't even reach his chin. He picked me up and threw me over his shoulder so that I was staring at the backs of his legs. With that, he walked me out of the room like I was a small bag of potatoes. I silently begged him to never put me back down.

Our cab pulled up to our destination for the evening. The club was, for lack of a better term, wild. It had just opened last week and was filled from wall to wall with women in skimpy dresses and men trying to come up with ways to end the night with those dresses on their bedroom floors. I hadn't been to a club since college and was rusty when it came to dancing and nightlife, in general. So, my first stop was the bar, and after three shots of cheap whiskey, I went to find my new friends. How many was that, now? Seven? I was determined to end my night with Luke, and I knew that I needed to be a little more forward to make that happen.

I laid eyes on him. He was standing next to Lana and Tom who were dancing, her back melting into his chest. As soon as Tom saw me, he moved Lana over and pulled me in for one of his bear-hugs. He was the kind of person who made everyone feel like his best friend.

"Brett! How wild is this place? I'm sweating like crazy. Do you want to go catch a breather outside, guys?" he said while trying to air out the arms of his t-shirt.

"No, dude, we're good! I want to dance, man. Brett, get over here," Luke said.

I quickly slid between them and began dancing with Luke, pushing myself into him. He spun me around and moved his hands from my waist around to the small of my back. He pulled me in to him, closely and firmly, and I threw my arms around his neck. Rising up onto the tips of my toes, I kissed him. Lightly and playfully, like dangling bait on a lure. And he bit. He kissed me back with such passionate intensity, it felt like we were the only two people on the entire planet let alone this crowded, sweaty room. Luke stopped me, traced my arm with his finger, and put his hand in mine, lacing his fingers between my own. He pulled me away from the dance floor. Tom and Lana kept dancing, but as he twirled her, I saw Tom follow us with his eyes as we walked toward the bar.

"Hey, Luke! Nice to see you, man." Of course, Luke knew the bartender. Who wouldn't want to know Luke?

"Four shots of whiskey," Luke said, "two for myself and two for this beautiful girl on my right." He smiled at me and winked, stroking my lips with his thumb.

Oh, man. I could have melted in that moment. I was the perfect amount of intoxicated. Too drunk to blush at this compliment and confident enough to grab Luke's face for another not yet sloppy make-out session. A groundbreaking moment of realization: Kurt hadn't been on my mind the entire night. I felt a mixture of guilt and satisfaction. Was I moving on too fast? I realized I honestly didn't care. He was probably off with the girl he deserted me for, and, in this moment, all signs were pointing towards Luke.

Luke.

"Alright, kid. Are you ready to turn the dial on this night all the way up to one-hundred?" He held both shots in his hand, cocked and at the ready.

"Well, that depends, Luke. Are you taking me home at the end of it?" He looked pleasantly surprised at my boldness.

"Oh, abso-fucking-lutely."

We threw back the shots. And that is the last thing I remember.

CHAPTER 7

I was awoken by a light so bright that I was sure it had burned out the irises of my eyes. My head was pounding like the bass of a giant stereo, and my brain felt like a shriveled raisin. I went to turn to the right of the bed, where my nightstand was, and grab a glass of cold water. My hand reached for air. My nightstand wasn't there. That was when I realized—I was not in my house. I turned to my left and saw someone sleeping next to me. It was Luke. He was breathing, slow and deep, still hibernating in a booze-filled slumber.

I checked my phone: two calls from Lana and a text from Phoebe. I opened Phoebe's text and got ready for a barrage of questions about my night, most of which I couldn't answer. What even happened?

Phoebe:

How did the rest of your night go?
You sounded WASTED when you called me!
And Luke said hi, too.
Did you end up going home with him?

Me:

> Uh. Wish I could tell you
> that I even remember the call,
> but I don't at all, LOL.
> But, yeah, I'm with Luke.
> He's still sleeping right next to me.

Phoebe:

> NO WAYYYYY!
> How was the sex?!
> Details NOW!

I took a moment to try and remember literally anything about the previous night. Last memory I could recall, we were taking shots. Did we even have sex? I looked under the sheets. I was naked, so fair assessment that we at least fooled around. Then I looked to my right on the floor: a condom wrapper. Well, shit, at least we knew to be safe.

Then a flash of a memory hit me, like a snapshot from a polaroid camera. Pictures, lots of them, spread out on the floor. A tile floor, it felt cool on my bare legs. And then I remembered: Luke had taken out a box of old photos from his closet. He wanted to show me pictures of his friends and family, and I had loved that he wanted to show me a little glimpse of his life. How humanizing this activity had made him, like he was just a normal guy and not this unattainable being.

Next thing I knew, it was all coming back to me. How I had taken the pictures out of his hands and led him to his room. How he had slowly slipped me out of my bra, kissing my chest as he followed the curves of my body with his fingers. How he gently pulled on my hair, tilting my head back ever so slightly so he could kiss my neck. How I had tugged him onto the bed and on top of me, trying to take a moment to memorize every inch of his body. But he had quickly slid his hand underneath me, between the sheets and the small of my back, and slid himself inside of me. I may not have been able to remember it all, but I knew that waking up next to that man was an ecstasy in itself. I hadn't felt like that in years. Luke rolled over towards me.

"Good morning, gorgeous. How did you sleep?" He pulled me into his arms.

"Good," I said, "but my head is killing me."

"Yeah, me too. I'll get us some water. Stay right here." He kissed me on the cheek and, entirely naked, got up to head to the kitchen. I couldn't help but stare, he was so perfectly tanned.

He lived alone which was nice. Just us two in our own little world inside these light grey walls. A robotic vacuum turned on in the far corner of his room. He was clean, too. He came back with a glass of ice-cold water, the condensation pooling on its outer rim. I greedily downed the entire cup in seconds.

"So, I have to get to my parent's house to help them out with some lawn work. But maybe I can see you sometime this week?" he asked.

"Hmm, like a date?" I inquired. *Shit*, too forward?

"Yeah, like a date. Unless you have another man and I'm stepping on some toes?"

I realized I had not told any one of my new friends about my broken engagement, and how my cancelled wedding was supposed to be in just a few weeks' time.

"Nope, super single and very open for a date," I said, probably sounding far too eager still.

"Alright, kid. I'll call you."

He kissed me one last time, helped me find all my clothes which had been strewn across the apartment, and called me an Uber. Such a gentleman, I thought. At least I found a great guy after having my soul crushed by one that was not so concerned for my well-being. I still hadn't heard from Kurt, but it didn't matter. I just wanted him to come pick-up the rest of his shit so that I could be rid of him. I didn't want this stage of my life to drag on any longer than it needed to.

When was he going to come by? He said he would. He needed his things. His clothes.

God, they still smelled so much like him. You know how everyone has their own, unique scent? No cologne can cover that up, not really. It stays. It permeates. The whole house was attempting to cleanse itself of that smell. To purify. To decontaminate.

~

A few days passed. Well, I guess it was a week. Everything was kind of blurring together for me lately. I found it exceedingly more difficult to focus on work. During every meeting I actually made it to, I caught myself daydreaming about my night with Luke. The taste of his skin, the feeling of his lips, the ridiculously attractive smile he flashed me whenever we looked into each other's eyes. At least twice I was told by my boss, Cheryl, to "focus up." Embarrassing, but warranted.

There was a new book she had wanted me to read, something redundant that she wasn't going to waste her time with. As her intern that was my burden to bear, and I had been slacking on it. And if I wasn't slacking on work due to fantasizing about being back in Luke's bed, I was checking my phone every five minutes for a text from him. It was torture, wondering when I would hear from him. He said he would call and that we would be going on a date. Not just a one-night stand, but more than that. Maybe even a boyfriend. I knew I was getting ahead of myself, but I couldn't just seal off my heart because it had some structural damage. I didn't want to swear off men and wind up fifty, single and a crazy cat lady.

By the time Friday rolled around and I hadn't heard from him, I texted Lana.

Me:

> Hey, girl! Any plans for this weekend?

Lana:

> Hey, babe!
> Yeah, Tom and I are thinking about having
> a little get-together tonight.
> Would you want to come??

Me:

> Yeah, definitely! Who's on the list?

Lana:

> Well, apparently Tom and Luke got into it –
> something stupid I'm sure.
> They argue like brothers.
> But, don't worry, I'll invite Luke for you.
> We saw you leave with him the other night.
> I want to know EVERYTHING when I see you!

Me:

> Haha, well, you know as much as I do.
> I kind of blacked out and just woke up
> in his bed the next day.

Lana:

> AH!! Amazing.
> Always good to get a casual fucking in!
> See you tonight, babe!

Tom and Luke were fighting? That was odd, they seemed so close. But that didn't concern me as much as what Lana said at the end of our conversation. "Casual fucking"? That is the last thing I wanted, especially with Luke. But that was just something Lana would say: she was a little bit of a wild child. In fact, in that moment I remembered another snippet from last weekend. I went to the bar by myself towards the end of the night to close out my tab. A guy came up to me and was standing so closely that I was under a barrage of his smoker's breath. As I was waiting for the bartender to return my credit card, he asked me to come home with him.

"No, thanks. I'm kind of here with someone so..." I looked around for back up. I didn't want to cause a scene, but I wanted out of that situation. Fast. In that moment, Lana came up to find me.

"What's going on here?" she asked him while eyeing him up and down. She looked like she needed an excuse to lose her temper.

"*Psh*, nothing. Your friend's just a cunt," he said as he finished his beer and left some cash on the bar.

As he turned our way to leave, Lana slapped him so hard that he thought she had punched him. He just stood there, mouth gaping open in surprise, with his hand on his stinging cheek.

"No one talks to her that way! Fuck off, you piece of shit! Go tug on your limp dick," she screamed at him while he was stumbling away. She and I laughed about the bright-red imprint of her hand that would be on his face for the rest of his night. She'd had my back. I was so grateful for my new little spit-fire friend. I was grateful for all three of them, truly. I couldn't imagine how hard this all would have been if I were still here in this city alone.

Even though I was a bit annoyed that I hadn't heard from Luke all week, I assumed he was just busy at work. He was in real estate, and I knew those hours were demanding and not exactly nine to five. So, I spent the evening smoking a few more of the joints I had rolled throughout the week and watching old movies. It was calm, but I found myself still struggling with the sensation that someone was sitting on my chest. I'd been feeling like that more often than not lately. What the hell was going on with me?

I glanced over to the spot under the bed, the one that housed Kurt's writings. Those painful yet honest words he had written. In that moment, I realized that I had to forget Kurt for so many reasons. But the only one that mattered was this: I wasn't letting him go, because he was never really mine to begin with. I never knew the real Kurt. All I knew was a silhouette of a man who was filled with secrets.

It was dark now, and I needed to get ready for the party. I moved slowly: I may have overdone it on the weed, I said to myself. I felt nervous, that same feeling you get before you do something like present a project to a classroom of judgmental students. What was this? I had never experienced this constant state of fear before. No, not fear. Worry. I unlocked the deadbolt on the door and turned the lock. Leaning my face outside, the humid breeze left me feeling sticky. Hot. Uncomfortable. Why did I open the door? Did I hear something? My heartbeat sped up. My chest was heavy. Was I breathing? Quickly, I closed the door and moved to lay back down on the bed. My bed.

Alone.

I promised myself that first thing tomorrow morning, I would start looking to rent a new place. Maybe I would find a private apartment on the thirteenth floor of some high-rise in the middle of downtown, like Lana. Clearly by his lack of communication since the breakup, Kurt wouldn't be coming back into my life.

Kurt.
No.

I needed to start somewhere new where I felt safe, with a code to access the lobby and a doorman to vet all those who entered. I needed to know who was around me. Plus, being close to my new friends and the excitement of downtown sounded like a no-brainer. This thought was the last one I had before I must have fallen asleep. I was awoken by a missed phone call from Lana.

It was 10 p.m., and I was late. I pulled the dress I'd laid out earlier that day onto my body. Wow, this fit more tightly last time I wore it. How much weight had I lost? Fleeting thoughts. I opened the Uber app on my phone and sent my request for a ride. As I waited, I stood in front of the mirror. Had my wish worked, that night on my birthday? Was this my painting? That girl in the mirror looking back at me seemed…tired. Sunken. Hopefully, the mirror held this version of me, and this mirror alone.

The app dinged. My ride was here. This alert broke the spell under which I was held while gazing in the reflective glass. I pulled away from it and grabbed my purse. Stepping outside, I felt better. Clear. I placed myself in my Uber and was on my way to the party. I may never have heard from Luke, but the idea of being back in his arms and surrounded by friends was like a warm bath. The rush of adrenaline leaving my system had put me in a dream-like state. I promised myself then when Luke arrived, I'd ask him if we could just ditch the party and go back to his apartment. This time, I'd be sober enough to remember.

CHAPTER 8

walked into Lana's and Tom's that evening feeling nervous. Luke having never called me for our date, I was beginning to question if I had done something wrong. Should I have texted him first? But I didn't have his number. Our first night together was more than sex – at least to me. I thought he felt the same way. Filled with uncertainty, I moved through the kitchen and past people I'd never met to find Lana. It was the kind of kitchen you'd see in the crisp folds of a home decorating magazine. Ornamental vases that housed no flowers, inscribed cutting boards that had never been used, salt and pepper shakers that held neither salt nor pepper. All these items meant to illustrate a picture-perfect life. I knew she wanted to get into politics, she was the president of her sorority. But this level of staging felt excessive. Why was she trying so hard? I was staring at the "Live, Laugh, Love" decals above the sink when Tom found me.

"Hey! So, it's a little wild in here. Lana and I are on the couch. Follow me," he said, grabbing my hand and leading me through the chaos.

As I passed by the partygoers, I searched for Luke. Tom sat me on the light green couch across from Lana and sat next to her on their love seat.

"Brett! I'm so happy you came!" Lana squealed. "Here – take a shot. I knew how much you love your *whissskey*," she sang the last word, handing me a small glass that was overflowing with brown liquid.

"You know me too well, Lana," I said, throwing the shot back. "What are you guys doing on the couch?"

"Well, it's easier to do blow when you're sitting down," she said, laughing.

Though still gracious, she nearly sounded a bit blunt tonight. Short, even. Was there a mocking in her tone?

"Luke's coming back with some plastic cups so we can play beer pong. Want a bump?" she asked in passing, almost bored.

So, Luke was here. At mention of his name, I felt that sensation again; like something heavy was sitting on my chest. Why was I so on edge tonight? Trying to numb this feeling, I quickly snatched the little plastic bag from Lana's hands. I placed a line of the snow-white powder on the grimy glass table. Using a plastic straw that I found in a cup to my left, I snorted the coke. It must have been more than I was used to, because I instantly found myself disoriented and tense. I rubbed the remains on my gums. Man, I felt like I was back in college.

In that moment, I saw Luke walking up behind Lana.

Luke.

He looked incredible, wearing a crisp, black button-down shirt tucked into a pair of clean, black dress pants. He must have come from showing a house. I wanted to be back in his apartment with him, alone but for the sound of our shallow breathing. Mid-reverie, I noticed that Luke was not unaccompanied. He was standing next to a tall, dark-haired woman. She was striking: perfectly curled hair that crept down to her waist, olive-colored skin that shone against her white dress, and deep, brown eyes. Wide, and the shade of chestnuts. I felt my stomach turn.

"Alright, I have the cups, but we may need to run out for more," he paused and smiled when he saw me.

"Hey, kid. Want to be my partner for beer pong?"

"Yeah, I just need to run to the bathroom," I said, shooting a glance Lana's way.

"Oh! Um, yeah! I'll come with you," she said.

I was thankful that she had gotten the hint. She gave Tom a kiss as she stood up from the couch. She side-stepped a bit as she moved towards me. Tom's usual wide-brimmed smile looked uneasy.

As we walked to the bathroom, arm in arm, I stole a glance behind me. I noticed Luke whisper something into the beautiful girl's ear. She threw her head back in laughter and delicately placed her hand on his arm. Who was the girl and why did he bring her here? Lana and I finally found our way into the bathroom. A framed picture of a mountain sat above the towel rack. It encouraged me, mockingly, to "never give up," with glittery, pink lettering. Fuck you, I silently told it.

"Okay, so you have to tell me what happened with Luke," Lana said, checking her makeup in the mirror, not even tossing a glance my way as she did.

"I mean, obviously it doesn't matter. Who the hell is that girl he brought?"

I sounded more distressed than I had wanted to. These people might be my friends, but I was new to the group, and I was certain that her allegiance lie with Luke.

"Oh, yeah, that's just his friend Gita. They work together. Apparently, she's kind of, like, his mentor. She kicks ass in the real estate world, obviously. I mean, *look* at her! I'd buy a house from that body," she said, barely breathing between words. I could tell she'd been indulging in her little plastic bag all night.

"Oh, so they're not dating or anything?" I asked, hopeful.

"*God*, no! Luke doesn't date. They've just hooked up a couple times. So, tell me about the other night! I hear he's *wild* in bed," she said, nearly vibrating.

In that moment, I didn't hear her words. I was trying to process all the information I had received from her drunken rambling. So, not only was Luke never planning on calling me for a date, he was fucking other people. I had fallen for the age-old trap: a player masquerading as a decent guy. I was entirely disappointed in myself. No, I was disgusted. After everything I had just went through with Kurt, I was stupid enough to open up my heart even the slightest bit to someone I barely knew.

Kurt.

Fuck.

It was my own fault, and I silently promised myself that I would never make that mistake again.

"Yeah, I mean, I'm sure it was a good time. I don't know. I was pretty hammered, so I don't remember much. Let's go back. Mind if I get another bump, first?"

"Yeah, sure," she said, now tussling her hair.

She handed me her little plastic bag and I stuck my nail inside. The color of its contents shone brighter against the matte black of my polish. Bringing the white powder to my nose, I felt invincible for a split second. We left the bathroom to rejoin the party. As we approached the couch, I noticed that Gita and Luke were sitting very closely on it. He had his arm resting upon her perfectly tanned shoulders. I saw two full shots of liquor on the table. I threw them back, one after the other.

"Woah, trouble is here. Brett, are you good?" Luke asked me, a little unease in his voice.

Fuck your concern, I thought.

"Yeah, man. I'm here to party. Are we playing a game or what?" I may have said this more aggressively than I intended.

"Luke, we need to be at the showing early, remember?" Gita said while fixing the collar of his shirt. I saw the way she looked at him. Approval? No, desire.

How intimate of an action. Obviously, they'd slept together. I felt insignificant, the size of the transparent shot glass I had placed back on the table.

"Yeah, I think Gita and I are going to take off. We have an open house tomorrow morning, and I need to prep. Thank you, guys, for having us over," he said in Lana and Tom's direction. "See you around, Brett. Enjoy your night and your whiskey."

As he went to leave, Tom locked eyes with him, and shook his head. Luke, clearly unphased by whatever Tom was disappointed in him for, flashed him a smile. He walked with Gita towards the front door. Right before they exited through it, I saw him grab her ass.

"You know, guys, I think I'm going to head out too. I'm feeling a little worn down," I said, trying not to make it obvious that I was on the verge of tears.

"Brett, no, don't leave! The night is just getting started – it's only midnight!" Lana said. Fuck, midnight *was* starting to seem early.

"Lana, can you grab us some waters?" Tom asked her.

He could tell I was upset. She looked his way. Her face betrayed zero emotion. She must be smashed, I thought. She turned to me, smiled, finished her drink in one giant gulp, and got up to head to the kitchen. Tom moved to sit in the chair next to me.

"Listen," he said, "Luke is an asshole. He does this – finds pretty girls who easily fall for his bullshit. I'm not saying you're naive or anything – I know you're smart and have a good head on your shoulders. It's just… rare that a girl doesn't buy into all that. I'm sorry, I should have warned you. But he moved fast."

"No, it's fine. I'm not upset," I lied. "I didn't, like, have feelings for him or anything. It was what it was: a one-night stand." Saying those words made me feel dirty. I wanted to shower off the sensation of being used.

"Yeah, but you're not one of those stupid girls he finds downtown. You're different. You're smart and fun and you don't deserve that fucker leading you on like that. I could see it in your eyes that you were into him," he said, an apology lining his words.

"Thanks, I appreciate that. I guess I fell for it a little. I don't really… sleep around, so, I guess I thought there was something more here. Either way, it doesn't matter. I'm just happy I have you and Lana. You two have really been good friends to me these past couple of weeks," I said. And I meant it.

It made me feel so cared for, Tom trying to look out for me. He was quickly becoming someone I could trust. Lana was all about showing me a good time and was the feminine energy I needed as a single girl looking for wild nights out on the town. But the friendship I had with Tom appeared to be deeper than that. He was the male friend I was missing in my life. Someone who would make sure that I was emotionally sound. He protected me like I was his sister. I guess losing my little brother, Morris, had always steered me in a direction to fill that void. And, Tom even came to my defense over his own best friend. That has to mean he saw me in the same light. Isn't that what brothers do?

Lana came back with two waters for just Tom and me. She clearly wasn't looking to slow down the party anytime soon.

"Look, Brett – don't leave. Forget about him and stay and party with us. Don't just sit at home on a Friday night," Tom said.

"You're upset about Luke?" Lana asked, looking a bit annoyed. I was bringing down her mood, and that was inexcusable.

"No, not at all. I'm just tired, Lana. You guys have fun! I'll see you next weekend?"

"Absolutely! We'll let you know what our plans are. You are *always* welcome," Tom said. So incredibly kind.

Lana waved me a haphazard goodbye and stood up to find a less serious group of people to spend her night with. It should have hurt my feelings that she didn't take a moment to make sure that I was alright. But I didn't care. I was so hurt by how the night unfolded, I just wanted to sit at home and try my hardest not to think. About anything. I wanted to go to sleep and not wake up until no one was on my mind.

Not Kurt.
Not Luke.
Not anyone.

The same strange sensation hit me once again. I couldn't take a deep breath, and my chest was tight. It felt like a string was wrapped around my ribcage, over and over again, with no give to allow my lungs to fill with air. My heart was racing. Clearly this feeling was getting worse. I decided that I would call my doctor on Monday to make an appointment. Maybe I had low iron. I still wasn't eating. I got out of the Uber, walked inside my little house and lay in a tiny ball upon my king-sized bed. It felt big. Too big. The covers upon my small body made me feel entirely unimportant. Like I could disappear within them, and no one would come looking for me.

No one would notice that I was gone.

I was allowing my eyelids to shut, closing myself off from the world, when a sudden feeling of urgency washed over me. Kurt's notebook. I checked under the bed for its brown leather cover. Worn and weathered. Its pages held the whole of a man who was only bits and pieces to me now. I realized: I may never be this close to his paper world again. Soon, he would come for the rest of his possessions. I brought out my cellphone and took pictures of the poems that I had read weeks ago. The ones that had both captivated and haunted me with their language. I still did not know for whom those poems of adoration were written and even though I was sure they were not about me, I could pretend. I could hold on to these screenshots as a sort of fabricated proof for myself: that someone did love me once. Even if they discovered that they loved someone else even more.

CHAPTER 9

By the time Monday had arrived, I was constantly plagued by the same incessant feeling of being suffocated. It was terrifying. Like a heavy, iron weight was sitting on my ribs. I never knew when the sensation would come on. It was totally unpredictable. That was the scariest part. After it hit me in the middle of a meeting that morning, I decided I'd had enough. I was able to book a same-day appointment with my general practitioner. Apparently, chest pain is a decently high-risk complaint.

Upon arrival at the doctor's office, I felt like I was on the verge of passing out. Everything felt surreal: I couldn't focus on my surroundings and I felt like my legs weighed nearly one hundred pounds, each. Even with that extreme, grounding weight, I couldn't stand on them. They wanted to buckle, they wanted to fold into themselves. As the nurse shuffled me through the lobby towards the examination rooms, she must have noticed that I was dazed.

The room was spinning.
My vision had begun waning.
I couldn't feel my hands.
My feet.
My face.
My head was losing blood.

My whole entire body was teeming with pins and needles, like when you sit on your leg for too long and it starts to ache.

Was I having a heart attack?

How?

I was only twenty-six.

"Are you feeling alright, sweetheart?" she asked. I watched her through the corner of my eye move to place the back of her hand on my forehead.

I was perspiring.

I barely felt her hand.

Everything was going dark.

Why wasn't she freaking out, too?

"Yeah, sorry, fine. I think…getting sick," I whispered.

I could feel my legs giving out
as I walked into my assigned room.
I was about to throw-up.
What was happening to me?

"Okay, just wait here. I'm going to bring the doctor in right away," she said as she hustled right back out to the hallway after she finished taking my vitals.

I wished she'd stayed.

I was scared.

Pins.

Needles.

When would she be back?

I felt extremely alone.

Alone.

The room was spinning.
I had to lay down.
A few seconds.
A minute.
Breathe.
Better.
My lips weren't tingling, now.
What *the fuck* was happening to me?
I *really* felt like I was dying.

A man entered less than a minute later.

"Hello there, Brett. How are we feeling today? Nurse Annie says not so well."

"Hi, Doctor. Um, yeah, I'm not… quite sure what's, um, happening to me. Lately I've been feeling really… shitty. I, uh, actually kind of can't breathe right now," I said through shallow gulps of overly sterilized air.

"Well, we're going to check this little reader I've placed on your arm in a minute, see what it says. Do you have a history of heart trouble?" he asked. He wasn't looking at me. Just at the machines.

Deep breath.
Beep.
Buzz.
Exhale.

I shook my head. "No history. In good shape. I run," I said, still sounding like a caveman learning language. Catching my breath was proving difficult, even with the added comfort of a doctor present in the room.

"Okay, well your vitals indicate that your heart rate is a tad elevated. Blood pressure isn't what it should be, either. And it also looks like you've lost a decent amount of weight recently, according to your chart. Have you ever struggled with anxiety in the past?" he asked while he checked my neck and abdomen.

Stethoscope.
Ice.
Shivers.

"Uh, not really. If I have a big meeting coming up at work. That what this is?" I was still struggling with my breathing, slowly gaining back the ability to take long, deep inhales. I was feeling the sensation come back to my toes and fingertips.

"Well, you know, panic attacks can present themselves as chest tightness. They can even feel like a heart-attack. You've just had a pretty decent one. But, nothing to worry about, Brett. We can prescribe you something for that. Easy fix," he said.

Don't worry.
Easy fix.
Fix.

I didn't understand how he was so nonchalant.

This wasn't anxiety.
This wasn't nervousness.
This was something fucking terrifying.

"So, you're saying this could keep happening to me?" I was panicked by that possibility.

"It could, but I'm going to prescribe you some clonazepam. Anytime you feel this coming on, I want you to take one. They're low dose, just 0.5 milligrams. You can take two a day," he said, as he wrote out the prescription. "Just don't mix it with alcohol."

And just as swiftly as he'd entered it, he was out the door. I was left with a piece of paper in my hands. Clonazepam. I looked it up on my phone. Class of drug: Benzodiazepines. Xanax? The shit rappers and bored housewives ate like candy? I left the office as quickly as my shaky legs could carry me. I went to the pharmacy, filled my prescription with no questions asked, and left with a tiny bottle filled with sixty little, yellow pills in my hand. They're so small, I thought. But they would fix me. I held onto them like they were flakes of gold. They were going to stop my body from betraying itself again. I drove home, feeling like I had solved the problem, and I'd barely had to put in any effort at all. Easy. Easy fix.

By the time 9 p.m. had rolled around, I was feeling overwhelmed. I had been so busy finding every avenue possible to ignore the break-up with Kurt that I'd neglected to actually deal with it at all.

Kurt.

I thought about him too much when it happened. Luke helped me forget.

Luke.

But then Luke was no longer my beautiful distraction. What would be a healthy means, I wondered? I realized that I hadn't spoken to my parents in days. I'd answered the daily texts from my mother. Her scheduled check-ins to make sure that I was adjusting to Kurt's absence in a healthy manner. She didn't want to smother me. She knew it would only make me retreat even deeper into my shell. Other than those quick conversations, I had been handling this pretty privately. I'd barely reached out to anyone. It was just how I dealt with life's obstacles. I didn't lunge over the hurdles, gracefully. I found a means to meander around them. Or, I would consume something that made them simply disappear. Poof, like a damaged magician. It probably wasn't healthy to handle this heartbreak with booze as my remedy. I dialed my mother's cellphone number. Hearing her voice, I realized that I had needed this more than I'd thought.

"Hey, honey. How are you holding up?" she asked. I could feel her through the phone.

Gentle.
Sunny.

"Hi, mom. I'm okay. Not really doing much, just working and hanging out with some new friends. How are you and Dad doing?" I had zero interest in disclosing my recent destructive behaviors. I'd partially been sidestepping them for that reason.

"Oh, we're fine, sweetie. Your father says he is signing you up for a dating site and hopes that an age range of seventy to eighty works. Don't worry, I'll smack him for you," she said mid-laugh.

Her laugh.
She was so pure.

I realized just how weird their sense of humor had gotten over the years. They were nearing seventy years old, somehow. To me, they were still that couple that ran a successful, albeit stressful, restaurant my whole life. They never stopped. They were still the most formidable forces on this planet, that would never change.

"Yeah, tell him if they're not on their death bed, I'm not interested. Men suck – I want easy money," I said, sighing at that half-truth.

"Ah, so the dating world isn't what you remember, huh?" she inquired.

"Eh, it's not worth talking about. How are the birds up there in the North Carolina home?" I asked her.

Avoidance.
Still my greatest talent.

My father and I called my mother "The Bird Lady" because of her obsession with them. Last time I'd checked with my dad, he had informed me that she had planted birdfeeders all across their back yard. His most recent count was about twenty. We teased her for this hobby, but in reality, she knew as much about the birds that visited their home as an ornithologist. She'd always been interested in birds. They amazed her. I wondered when that started. What began her fascination? I'd have to ask her one day.

Suddenly, I heard my dad's voice.

"How are you doing, monkey girl?" he asked.

It was his nickname for me when I was small and used to spend my days climbing onto his shoulders. He couldn't bear to part with it. It would just be confirming what he already knew to be true: I was too big now to rest there. That I was too old now to need my dad. The first may have been true but the second never would be. God, they deserved more children to love.

My brother.
Morris.
Not now.

My dad had actually saved my life once. When I was around 5 years old, a prisoner had broken out of a local jail and assaulted two women in search of a working getaway car. He was high on crack and needed to escape the authorities who were hot on his tail. It was in that moment that this man jumped the bushes of a woman's yard and was sprinting toward our family car. It was a nice day outside. Spring in Florida. My dad had parked the car, gotten out and was about twenty feet away, chatting with a neighbor. I was alone in the backseat of the car. I still remember seeing this man racing toward me: the look of pure panic in his every feature. The man was in the car instantly, almost like he'd always been there. In my memory, he always would be there.

He was failing in his attempt to work the stick-shift. I was small, but I was kicking his seat and screaming with all the power my tiny lungs possessed. I knew he was a bad man, especially when he told me to "shut the fuck up!" He couldn't have been in the car for more than a few seconds before my dad reached the driver's-side door. My dad pried the door open and jumped inside the car with the man, struggling to yank the gearshift from his trembling hands. He begged the strung-out man: "Just take the car but leave my daughter," he pleaded, "you can have the car. Please, she's my only child." Realizing the man wouldn't do so willingly, he summoned all of his strength, pulled the man out of the car and away from his little girl. He had him pinned on the ground by the time the cops showed up. Apparently, this all happened in seconds. To me, it was hours.

On that day, my dad became my own personal superman. He was my hero. I would always need him.

"I tried to tell your mother that you needed some time up here with us. That would help you, wouldn't it? I really don't like you living alone, especially in that house. I mean, your mom needs a new companion – she's started talking to the birds. Even scarier – she thinks they're talking back." He was also a natural comedian and missed having me around to be his one-woman audience.

"Well, you married her, dad. Honestly, if I came up there, I wouldn't be much help. I would probably just sit and talk to birds with her," I said. "It sounds peaceful."

Peaceful.

It would be a child-like security to be held in my mother's arms. To hear her tell me that everything would be okay. It would be comforting to hear my dad say that no man deserved me and that he would take care of his baby girl. But he couldn't rush me to the hospital for this type of injury. This wasn't a pain that an emergency room doctor could diagnose. There was no broken bone to set. This was an inner wound, and one that I was fixing just fine with booze, weed and blow. I didn't want them to worry about me, and they would if they could see how frail I'd become in such a short amount of time.

What I needed was someone my age who could abuse themselves with me. A confidant, but one who couldn't just abandon me because my grief was a bit of a bummer. I ached like half of me was missing. *They* didn't just need another child to love. *I* needed a sibling. *I* needed my brother. But he was buried at the cemetery in a cocoon of dirt and decay. This time, I couldn't stop my mind from conjuring up that disturbing image. Instantly, my chest felt strangled.

No.
Not now.

"Hey, so, I need to run. I have a meeting tomorrow and I need to prepare. Tell mom I said bye. I love you both, okay?" I hung up the phone.

As incredible as it was to hear their voices, my parents couldn't stop this feeling from hundreds of miles away. The room was spinning as I searched my purse for the little, yellow saviors. I remembered what the doctor had said: they were low-dose and I could take one up to two a day. I hadn't even taken my first, so I figured what's the harm in doubling up the dose? A panic attack was approaching, and I would rather knock myself out than experience it again, full force. So, I took the clonazepam and I let myself fall upon the bed.

I waited a few minutes for the tablets to do their job. I realized I had no idea what to expect. Am I supposed to feel any different? Waiting for them to do their job gave me almost as much anxiety as did my life.

But then they kicked in. Oh, did they kick in.

They came on
slowly,
tiptoeing their
way through my
veins.
A wave of peace
rushed over me,
as if my body was
at a forcible
cease-fire with
itself.
All the
weapons were
lain down.
I felt my body
relax,
inch by inch,
like it was
being gently
lowered
into warm
water.

Every part of me was serene.
I had never known a calm this powerful.
The chemicals penetrated my entire being.
Mind, body and soul.
I couldn't feel stress.
My chest was open.
I could breathe.

I inhaled all the beauty I felt in this moment, deeply and freely.

I exhaled all the pain of the past few weeks.

I was transformed.

I felt *nothing*.

These little, yellow pills had saved me. I silently said a prayer of thanks to the pharmacists. Feeling like I was a balloon slowly gaining more and more helium, I searched the covers for my phone. In its black mirror, I caught a glimpse of my reflection. Hi, Dorian. I was smiling for no reason. The absurdity of it made me giggle like a little kid. I dialed Phoebe on FaceTime.

"Hey, dude! How was the party? Why are you smiling like an idiot?"

"*Maaaaan* fuck the party, Luke's a dick. Doesn't matter though, I went to the doctor.

Turns out I have anxiety, *but* he gave me bars and now I feel *greaaattt*." I saw my picture in the left corner. Smiling. Happy.

"Wait, what? You're kind of slurring your words, Brett. You went to the doctor?"

"Yeah, but he fixed me. These pills, Pheebs. You have to try 'em. I feel *incredible*." Swinging the phone's camera, I showed her the pill bottle.

"How many did you take? Don't mess with those, dude. They're no fucking joke. I know people who have OD'd on those. Are you okay?" She looked too stressed. She needed these little tablets.

"Pshhh I'm fine. I only took two, okay? They're low dose. Doctor's orders, so I'm *good to gooo*."

"Alright, dude if you say so. So, what happened with Luke? He turned out to be a player? Man, I thought he was different."

"None of them are different, Pheebs. Everyone is the same. They leave before they can be bothered with human fucking emotion." I reminded the small icon of myself in the screen that I would never fall for that again.

"Well, that's not everyone, Brett. I would never leave you. I know you feel like life is shit right now, but *please* never forget that. I'm your sister, and I would never do that to you. You will *always* have me."

And I knew she meant that. I had at least one person in my life who would never break me. Phoebe would always be there, no matter what. Even in my numbed state, the thought of that made my eyes water.

"I know, Pheebs. I can count on you. You're my best friend and I promise I'm okay. Mostly because I've had you to lean on through this. Tell Seth I say 'hi.'"

"I will. Anything for you, Brett. You know that. Anyways, I've got to go make dinner.

Call me anytime with life-updates. And, seriously, fuck Luke. You don't need that garbage. You're self-healing right now. Focus on you."

So, she didn't like that I was taking benzos. I was drinking myself into oblivion and doing a decent amount of blow. I was making her nervous with my life decisions lately and I didn't want to push her away from me, too. Even worse, I didn't want her to make me stop. It all worked too damn well. The perfect combination.

But as I hung up the phone, I caught my reflection once again. This time it didn't reflect a blissful smile. What I saw in it was something dark. Something paranoid. Something destructive. I wasn't self-healing. I had done nothing but damage myself the past few weeks, from the inside out. I was self-sabotaging. And I couldn't continue on like that. I needed to care about myself the way those who loved me did. And I still had people who loved me.

Feeling insignificant in my full-sized bed, I pulled my legs up to my chest and wrapped my arms around my ankles. I cried for the part of me that I'd been so hell-bent on extinguishing. My heart may have been shattered but I could mend it. In that moment, I made the first step. I willed two tiny shards back together.

CHAPTER 10

stuck to my promise. I didn't take more than the doctor's recommended dose of clonazepam. One at a time. I drank less. Well, kind of. No more shots, at least. Less weed. And definitely no more blow. Not another full-on panic attack plagued me. Just minor feelings of unease. A low hum, an inner vibrating. I was recharging. I began feeling marginally restored. More like myself, if anyone can even say they know what that means. I started reading again. Charlotte Perkins Gilman. *The Yellow Wallpaper*. Weeks had passed before I finally took a moment to appreciate my improvement. It would take time to remedy the damage done. But I was taking a small step back from the edge of the cliff. The problem was that the call at the bottom of its pit stayed calling.

Nevertheless, I committed to bringing myself back to reality. I had been truly excelling at my job and I was relishing my time in the office. I remained on task. I began consistently bringing my work home. I went from famine to feast. I couldn't get enough. When at work, I spoke to colleagues. Small talk, nothing overly inviting. I was one of the youngest in the office and most of my coworkers had years of experience under their belts. My position was the bottom of the office food-chain. But I always possessed a passion for books that I think most of them lacked. I was driven to engross myself in work. Anything to keep myself busy. And my manager was noticing it. Cheryl pulled me aside after the usual Wednesday morning meeting to voice her approval of my new-found assertiveness.

"Brett, I wanted to chat with you for a second, can you come in my office?"

She looked happy, but I felt that familiar tickle in my chest. It's okay, I told myself. This is normal nervousness. I was able to talk myself down, now. Still, before I stood up from my chair in my pint-size cubical, I checked my purse for the pills. Just in case. They never left my side. I followed her inside of her office.

As I sat in the chair across from her desk, I waited impatiently for her to speak. I stole a glance out the window of her brightly lit, neutrally-toned workspace. Located on the ninth story of a Sand Lake office building, her office was an Orlando dream. I watched the I-4 freeway traffic zip by at warp speed.

"I'm really impressed with how much of an initiative you've taken lately," she said as she texted on her phone. I didn't take offense to her lack of attention. She was constantly multi-tasking. Just part of the job, I figured.

"Thank you so much, Cheryl. I was just… getting over a pretty shitty cold. But I'm back and I'm ready to make a name for myself here."

"Well, PubPave is really lucky to have you on the team. I wanted to let you know that we have a role that needs to be filled and I think you're the person for the job. How would like you like to be a junior publisher?"

I was in shock. It was the fantasy; all I had been working toward. I'd wanted to be a publisher since I was a young girl surrounded by Shakespeare in my parent's bookshop. How long had I been obsessed with books? This was my calling. But what if I wasn't ready? That same uncomfortable sensation washed over me for a second time. I instinctively reached my hand inside my purse once again.

"Wow, Cheryl, I am… ehm," I cleared my throat, "yes, I would *love* that!"

"Alright, well, you're my first choice. Keep up the hard work. Again, well done, kiddo."

She was out the door before I could respond.

I was floating on air the entire walk to my cubicle. I had stopped partying and started focusing on moving my life forward. Clearly, the universe was congratulating me for my progress. I began loving myself, gradually. My self-worth was still mildly in question; it seemed to depend on my ever-changing mindset. There were moments when I fell short. I spent many lonely nights sleeping next to an empty bottle of wine instead of a man. It was better that way. Safer.

Although bumps of cocaine were no longer on my mind, I had hung out with Lana and Tom a couple times since their party. We attended a few happy hours with low price appetizers and high-quality martinis. I was no longer compulsively throwing back shots in order to numb my pain. I was enjoying myself again. Slowly, I was regaining interest in food and I even put on a few pounds. I still looked weak, but at least I was improving. Even if it was slightly. One particular night out with the duo, we attended a special event at a restaurant downtown. Wine Wednesday. I met up with Tom and Lana, eager to spend some time with two people who had proved to be a welcome distraction for the past month. However, this night had proven to being quite the opposite. After a round of high-end mozzarella sticks and relatively shitty red wine, Lana asked me to betray my desire to remain entirely guarded. She requested that I open up about myself. I hadn't yet, I realized. They didn't know much about me. Honest conversation wasn't a part of our package. Specifically, she wanted to know who had fucked me up so terribly that I was resigned to a life of romantic semi-solitude.

"Okay, so, full disclosure – I was supposed to get married in about two weeks." I nonchalantly took a sip of half-priced chianti.

"No way! Brett, holy *shit*! Who's the guy? What happened?" Lana probed. She looked like she'd been starved for gossip and had been given a massive fix all at once.

"Dude, ignore her," Tom said, grabbing a piece of fried cheese. "Don't go into it if you don't want to. I imagine that was a pretty traumatizing life experience," he said with a comforting touch of his hand to my own.

Lana looked like she was ready to storm away from the table. But then she flashed a forced smile and took a sip of her pink martini with a lime-sugar rim. She really was a natural politician with the way she buried unpleasant emotions. Anything to keep up appearances. I wondered why they had been so venomous with each other lately. Trouble in Lana's self-created paradise, I supposed.

"It's not like I'm asking for much," she said, throwing Tom a playful smirk. "But that's just pretty *wild*, you know? I didn't expect that. Just cold feet? Did someone cheat?" Lana was interviewing me, and I hated being her source of what felt like celebrity dirt.

"Nothing too exciting, okay? We just… fell out of love, I guess. Well, he did. I don't know, guys. I don't really want to get into it. But now you know. I'm just not interested in being hurt like that again, so, yeah, I've kind of sworn off dating for now." I hoped that was the end of this uncomfortable journey into my heavy baggage.

"Of course, Brett. No worries – it's not our business. We care about you and if you ever need to talk, we're here. Right, Lana?" Tom shot her a look. Not cute or playful.

I noticed irritation, maybe even a little disappointment in his eyes. What was going on with these two? I didn't want to be impolite, but I didn't want to be at the table any longer. I had my own issues to deal with, and their tension was palpable.

"Alright, well, I've got to go. My work has me prepping for a new role and I need to ace the interview. Lana, you can have the rest of my wine if you'd like?"

I was extending an unnecessary olive branch as a way to apologize for not giving her the gossip fix she was so craving. She was proving herself to be a superficial presence in my life. But beggars can't be choosers. I had no other close friends in Orlando to spend time with. At least Tom under-stood. He had begun texting me nearly every evening to ask about my day. One night, he opened up about the rocky coast his relationship had found itself marooned upon.

Tom:

I'm sorry Lana has been so shitty lately.
She's become so...selfish.
She just always has to know everything
that goes on in people's lives.

Me:

What do you mean?
Has she changed?

Tom:

You know what? No, she hasn't.
I think I'm just finally realizing that.
She gets mad at me for no reason.
I don't think she likes our friendship.

But that's all it was: a friendship. Neither one of us had even made it seem otherwise. Tom just had a higher emotional intelligence than most men. That didn't mean he was coming on to me. In fact, he had never even hinted at anything other than friendship.

Me:

> Oh. Well, she has to know
> that we're just friends.
> Obviously, you love her.
> I see the way you look at her.
> It's beautiful.

Tom:

> Of course, we're just friends.
> I do love her.
> I just need to do some damage control
> with the First Lady.
> Anyways, check in if you need us.
> Night!

The stress of causing strife between these two humans made that unwelcome sensation return to my chest. What was I doing wrong? I had been nothing but easygoing with them both. Enjoyable, even. I had said "yes" to nearly every invite, and there had been plenty. Why was Lana so irritated? I anxiously combed through my purse for the pill bottle. I was already halfway through the bottle, but in the last few days I had been taking them as the doctor ordered. Releasing one from its chamber, I dropped it upon my tongue. With a sip of water, I was on my way to rest. In that moment, my phone buzzed.

The name I read on the screen caused the breath to catch in my throat.

Kurt:

> Hey, Brett. I need to see you.

CHAPTER 11

panic-dressed into a pair of worn jeans and a band t-shirt. Checking myself in the mirror, I noticed that the shirt was from a concert we'd seen together. Blink-182. The only one he ever took me to. In the mirror, for just a moment, I saw us dancing in the aisles. His fingers laced in mine as he twirled me. The way he smiled at me. I was so happy in that moment—there may have been thousands of people around us but all I saw was him. Suddenly I was craving a twelve-dollar beer and slice of sub-par pizza.

Shaking the memory, I took a moment to look at my reflection. *Really* look at it. I was locking eyes with a stranger. Someone I wouldn't have recognized only a month ago. I watched the movement of my hand as it pushed my hair away from my face. This woman was so entirely unsure of herself. Just a few months ago, I had it all figured out. At least I *thought* that I did. In a few moments, I would see someone who I had nourished a relationship with for years. A man I loved. My almost-husband. Once, we knew each other like we knew ourselves. And yet I felt like I was being visited by a ghost in chains. I wondered what past sins I would be confronted with. What mistakes I would need to apologize for. What the future held for me if I didn't.

I stopped my anxious mind in its jumpy tracks. I owed him *nothing*. He was the one who fell in love with someone else. I had no skeletons in the closet that needed to be aired. I needed only to ask one simple question: why her? In that moment, I was thankful for the clonazepam in my system.

Suddenly, I heard a knock at the door. Two determined taps of knuckle to wood.

After a month of no contact, I was finally starting to let him go. I had started moving on, finding peace in all of this. It made me mad that I should be tested like this. Wrathful. After I pulled myself together, I opened the door.

And there he stood.

Seeing him in front of me, all my anger drifted away with the night breeze. I knew that I still loved him. Maybe I always would. It was as if I had merely placed my love for Kurt on a brief hiatus.

Kurt.

When he smiled at me, I knew that to be true.

"Hey," I said tersely, "you can come in. Everything is where it's always been. I have a bottle of wine on the counter," I said as I wandered toward the kitchen for two glasses.

"Thanks, I hope I'm not bothering you. I know it's late."

The way he slightly slurred the last sentence, I gathered that he was drunk. That's funny, I thought. One of his major complaints about his high school ex was when she showed back up at his parents' place, trying to work things out after their break-up, completely hammered. I didn't think he was trying to get back together. It was just ironic, I guess.

"Not a bother, Kurt. I'm glad you're here. It's actually really nice to see you." I meant it.

"It's nice to see you too, Brett. Wow, you really, you look great," he said.

I looked *great*? I had lost twenty pounds since he last saw me. Did he really not notice how frail I'd become?

"Um, yeah, thanks. Can't say I've been working out, so."

"Well, you do. Look great, that is."

We both paused. We just looked at each other. Tiptoeing. Each of us felt like we'd been dropped in a field filled with landmines. Neither of us knew where each other's bombs were set, and what would set them off. Kurt kicked his feet at a chip in the tile floor.

"So, where are you staying?"

I figured it was a rather innocuous question. Then I realized: it may not be. What if he was staying with *her*? Her.

"Oh, with my parents. My mom has been a wreck. She, uh, isn't too pleased with me."

"Well, she wanted us to stop living in sin, so I imagine she isn't too pumped about you being single again." I was fishing, but I hoped he hadn't caught on.

"Ah, well, nothing makes her happier than telling me how to live my life."

No information given. A closed book.

"Do you remember that one time that she tried to convince us to go to church with her on Sundays? She said we needed to 'reconcile with Jesus.'"

"Oh, God. Yeah, she tells me that a lot lately. I think she feels like I'm moving closer to the dark side daily. It was nice to have you as a buffer for that, not going to lie," he said shrugging. A small laugh escaped his lips.

It was nice to hear him say he missed having me around. But I guess he hadn't said that, had he? For a few moments, neither one of us spoke.

"So, how's work?" he asked nervously. He sat in chair at the table, slowly, easing his body into the wood.

As I prepared to answer him, I poured two glasses of wine. I was sitting across from him at our old table. The table on which we had shared so many meals. A memory crossed my mind, fleetingly. The night he made me hibachi that tasted identical to my favorite Japanese steakhouse, Kobe. He'd tried to flip the tail of my shrimp into his worn, FSU hat from college.

He'd completely missed. He smiled and bowed, proud of his attempt and placed the cap back onto his head. What happened to that comedian? I couldn't remember the last time we'd laughed together. And so, the memory had been doused with a reality check. I re-focused on the task at hand.

"Listen, Kurt, I'm trying to understand what you're doing here, to be completely honest with you. You said you 'needed to see me.' Why? We haven't spoken since you left," I said, determined.

"I know, I know. Look – I'm just going to be honest with you. I thought that I wanted this. I thought I needed time to figure things out. It just became... too much. The wedding was fucking *suffocating* me, Brett. I mean, fuck, I just needed an *out*. Can't you understand that?"

He was up from his chair and pacing across our living room carpet. *Mine*, damnit. I'm not going to detox him all over again, I thought. This conversation is over. It should be over.

"No, Kurt, I *don't* understand. Why the *hell* did you even propose to me in the first place? You didn't want this wedding from the start. You didn't help with *anything!* I did *everything* and then you finally fucking man-up and tell me you didn't want to get married *two months* before our wedding? It was humiliating, Kurt."

I never got to have my reaction and he was going to hear it now.

"I know, Brett. I know I was an asshole for waiting until the last minute. But I just... I don't know! It hasn't been easy for me either, okay?"

"Oh, *please* tell me how hard it's been for you. I dare you. Tell me how much you've suffered, Kurt. Tell me!"

I was crying and yelling between the tears. My composure had left me entirely.

"Look, I thought I wanted to marry you. Honestly, I did. You have to believe me. But I think... fuck, Brett. You just wanted me to propose *so badly*. I mean, we got into *fights* about it, don't you remember?"

And in that moment, I realized what I had done. How I was guilty here, too. I thought back to the months leading up to the proposal. How we'd gotten into a fight at my friend's wedding because I didn't understand why he hadn't proposed yet. How I had brought it up nearly once a month for a year after that. How every time a friend got engaged, and everyone showered their Facebook with celebratory words, I became envious. How my voice would emphasize the word "engaged" whenever I showed him the posts.

In the end, he proposed because he felt that he had to. He had weighed the options, and realized that if he didn't, he would lose me. He would lose his comfort zone. I really hadn't given him a choice. This realization broke me more than the breakup had. For how long was I manipulating what Kurt and I had into what *I* wanted? I had created my own little world. How long had I been trying to force him into a life he didn't want? He wasn't the problem. I was.

I was.

"I know there's nothing I can say to make you forgive me for that. I do love you, Brett. It was all just so … confusing. You have to believe me – I never stopped loving you!"

Those five little words rested between us, feebly floating through the soft air, searching for a place to land. We looked into each other's eyes. Mine were filled with a legion of questions. His were holding the answers he may never reveal. But in that moment, none of it mattered. The five little words had found a dwelling within my heart, and I leaped toward him. I was back in his arms. I was home.

Home.

I felt all the pain, stress, anger of the past month dissolve. All that mattered was the power in our embrace. The force of it. It was as if I was patch of dried sand being welcomed back to the sustaining calm waters of the ocean. Kurt was the nourishment I had been craving, and I finally felt safe in the shelter of his arms. Oh, how I had missed it.

When I moved my face to meet his eyes once again, I noticed that he was crying. I couldn't remember the last time I'd seen him express this basic human emotion. And then, he had stopped. This must be what it's like to witness Hailey's Comet, I thought. A quick flash, and then it's over. Not to be seen again in a lifetime. But I'd never forget it.

Without thinking any longer, I leaned myself into him and lightly pressed my lips against his. A curious brush, a request. Hesitantly and then with resolve, he surrendered his lips to mine. We kissed with the passion of a million words left unsaid. I didn't need to know about the girl from the poem. With this kiss, I could sense that for whatever reason, she no longer had a grip on his heart. She no longer mattered. Maybe she never did. Maybe she was always just a means of escaping a decision he no longer wanted. A poorly built excuse. Maybe, just maybe – all he ever wanted was to turn back time and merely exist with me. In that moment, I knew that was all we would ever require from each other.

Time.

We stumbled as we hastily moved our bodies to my bed. Our bed, once again. The thought permitted me to uncoil within myself all that had become so tightly would. He tugged at my t-shirt, peeling it off in one fluid movement. With this, I could breathe again. My chest was open. The air was so fresh, so renewed that I nearly felt greedy for pulling it into my lungs. For stealing it from the space between us.

We didn't yield a moment to fully comprehend what was happening. Kissing him hungrily, I moved my hands to the zipper of his jeans, freeing him from them. As I sat on the bed, my arms supporting me behind my back, he kneeled to the floor. He pulled my jeans down, quickly, almost too quickly. I wanted to savor every minute. My back on the sheets, Kurt laid his body on top of mine. His fingers slowly moved their way from my waist up to my chest. I gripped his arm, feeling his muscles moving as he touched me. As his hands roughly cupped the bottoms of my breasts, I noticed he wasn't looking at me. Not in my face, not in my eyes. I wanted to connect, I wanted to see him. I tried to move his head, lightly, my fingers leading his gaze towards mine. Instead, he tossed my body so that it was atop his, so that I was straddling his chest. He pulled my face down to his and kissed me with a passion so intoxicating that my mind went entirely blank. Finally, my thoughts surrendered.

We let ourselves be swept up in the passion of time lost and pointless apologies. Our figures found within each other all we needed in that instant: understanding. We were tiny vessels in a dimly lit room, and it was beautiful. He flipped me once again, sitting us both up, holding me as I rode him. As we thrusted against one another, I couldn't betray the moment with anything more than my bare body against his. I bit his shoulder, holding back every desire to whisper "I love you" as he continued to push himself inside of me. Any words would have been damaging. This wasn't about explaining ourselves. This was so much more than that.

After we finished, he rolled away from me and onto his back. Plagued with sweat, we each took a moment to breathe in the aftershock of what we'd just done. My mind was racing once again. I knew that our reconciliation would be difficult. We would need to consider what derailed us and find a new path to follow. One which cultivated communication. We needed to discuss the breakup and what would mend our relationship. I was about to initiate the first stages of this conversation.

I was stopped before I could begin.
"This was a mistake," he said.

And just like that, all the beauty of this moment between us vanished.
All the repairs I had made to my broken heart,
all the fragments I had mended,
were torn apart.
Any healing I had planted within myself
had been yanked out at the root.

CHAPTER 12

would like to say that I wasn't shocked. Truly. I even thought to myself: can I really blame anyone but myself for allowing this to happen? No, I couldn't. But hearing those words triggered a surprising pain, like a gunshot from an enemy I should have spotted. I was too busy enjoying a moment of peace in a war for which the purpose I never fully understood. I remained shell-shocked as he continued speaking through the chaos.

"Fuck. Oh, *shit*, I'm sorry. God, I shouldn't have come over," he said as he reached for his clothes.

"Asshole," was all I could mutter.

"I am a fucking asshole. I just needed to come and see you, to talk to you. I was feeling lost, Brett. I don't know who I am without you."

I sat quietly on the bed, staring at a small stain on the sheets. It was blue. What was that from? How long had it been there? Would it wash out?

"Look – I'm sorry. I know, *I know* I've been selfish. I just, I missed having someone who understood me. You always got me, Brett. I needed a fr—"

And with the first part of that word vibrating within my ears, I snapped out of my trance with a fury.

"*Don't* say friend. Do not even *dare* fucking call me your friend! *Friends* don't treat each other this way. Fuck if someone who *loves* you does, either."

I had started dressing myself and sat on our bed.

My god-damn bed.

Not this again.

I was fuming.

"Look, I get it! I'm so sorry. I just... *Jesus*, I can't do anything right. I don't know what I want and clearly I just keep fucking people over." He moved to leave. People?

"Who is she, Kurt?" I asked as I stood up to meet his gaze.

In that moment, finally summoning this courage, I felt much taller than five feet.

"What?" He turned pale.

"You heard me. I know there's someone else. I'm not a total idiot, except for allowing you to come back into this house."

"Brett, it's not what you th—"

"Oh, fucking *save it*, Kurt! You have never been honest with me, have you? I haven't been able to get a goddam *feeling* out of you since we met! I always thought that somehow, *somehow* it was my fault. But it was never about me. You're just always looking for the next person to heal you. To fix whatever the hell has got you so emotionally backed-up. Well, I'm not doing it anymore. Leave. *Now*."

As he turned to leave, he looked at me one last time. I saw the moment the lightbulb went on in his mind. I knew it had been lit as he recalled his notebook. His paper world. His writing had betrayed him. The ink on its fragile pages had bled, and his secrets had escaped the binding. Moving towards the bed, Kurt placed himself on his knees near its edge. He bent down to retrieve his confidant. He may have been mad that I read it. That now I knew what I had never been meant to understand. But his expression was merely one of suffering. I didn't know if he felt it for me or for himself.

Standing, I saw him consider for a moment. He went to open his mouth and quickly closed it. It was as if he was at a crossroads within himself. One part of him wanted to tell me everything. Maybe that was the part of him I fell in love with. But another part of him wanted to remain silent.

To shut me out once and for all. I had never witnessed his walls being built in real-time. But they were rising, and I felt them tower above me. I knew I would never be allowed to peak behind them again.

Kurt held on to his notebook tightly and with conviction as he moved toward the door. He placed his hand upon the handle and began to turn it. Then he paused. I'll never know what made him hesitate in that moment. Then, all at once, he pulled open the door and shut it behind himself. I no longer felt guilty for taking in the air that surrounded me. Any sacred air left was sucked out the door with his exit. I was left with the stagnant, foul air, a product of emptiness. He walked out on me a second time. I let him leave me twice. Because, in the end, this was my fault.

My fault.

Kurt, the Kurt I had shared a life with, was a construct. He was *my* paper world. Kurt was never who I imagined him to be. I had written his character in my life story to be whom I had wanted. I had loved an idea of a man from the start, and it was he who had faded away. The real Kurt was unattainable from the beginning. Our first conversation about our love for fiction was in itself a narrative. I thought he respected an author's talent to create when in reality, he was trying to tell me he loved it for the escape. He had proposed to me because it fit into my story. As the main character of my own life, I needed that next step. It was the next point of my plot, the continuation of the rising action.

I had turned him into a minor character from the beginning. He was static. It was cruel but it was easy. He never fought back, he never challenged me to allow him to write his own journey because he had grown so comfortable in the supporting role. Kurt had become a dynamic character just as the climax was visible. He cut our story short when he finally realized it was never our story to begin with, only mine. Honestly, in time, I may have admired this about him. But after he left our little home and me with no resolution, I only felt the sting of a highly anticipated story with a poorly written ending.

Ending.

But there was still an ending to compose. My tale would not be that of a damsel in distress rendered useless by yet another heartache. I had made the mistake of assuming that I could create the life I wanted from the one I had before me. I tried to mold a masterpiece from a flop. I misjudged my entirely disengaged college sweetheart as my story's main love interest. I'd also established Orlando as my proper setting merely because it was the place I'd lived in my entire life. I needed adventure. I wanted variation. I craved an unfinished book.

Unfinished.

I stopped for a moment to let myself feel the weight of being rejected a second time by the man with whom I had once wanted to spend forever. I waited for the tears to come. Five minutes passed, and all I felt was an odd sense of comfort. I didn't wait to analyze that unexpected feeling. I sprang into action, and fast. I sent out a group text to my college friend group and asked if I could come and visit them. All of them. I wasn't alone, not in the slightest. I had friends, close, dear friends, in so many different states. Places I'd never visited. See, after college we all moved across the country. I had been so busy trying to nourish a relationship that didn't deserve to be sustained that I had missed out on my early twenties. Time with friends.

People who shaped me.

Since Kurt had broken up with me in March, I had been participating in the harmful yet expected reactions of someone who regrets becoming newly single. I wallowed, I self-medicated, I rebounded. I was too deeply rooted in my "pity party" to notice that it was entirely unnecessary. I was free from a potentially loveless marriage! And I had nothing to give him except for the engagement ring.

~

The next month was spent in true *Eat, Pray, Love* fashion. Or, I imagine it was. I actually never read the book. It wasn't a classic and it sounded too cheerful. At the end of the following week, I asked my boss if I could use up the rest of my vacation time at work. Cheryl wasn't thrilled at first, but when I finally filled her in on my recent life trials, she wished me well and challenged me to not think about work or my "fuck-wad of an ex" for the duration of my three weeks off. I hadn't realized she was funny. She told me my interview for the junior publisher job could be held when I returned.

My first stop was to Tallahassee, Florida. During the day, Phoebe and I walked around our old college campus and reminisced about having picnics out on Landis Green. Then, at night, Phoebe took me out to enjoy all of our old stops for a classic undergrad Friday. We stopped at the Poor Pig's Bar and participated in "all you can drink." We passed through BJ's with its rooftop bar that was poorly built and would sway when enough people were dancing on it. She even dragged me into the Pantheon: the club where we used to do ecstasy while listening to EDM and wearing a ghastly amount of mismatched neon. We ended the night at our favourite pizza spot, GoGo's, with slices the size of our heads.

"Holy shit, Pheebs, I feel like I'm 21 again," I said in between bites of pizza so hot I was sure I'd feel the burns on my tongue if I wasn't so hammered.

"Well, we'd have done this a lot more before we graduated, but you and Kurt just wanted to stay in and get high most nights," she said while blowing on the magma-hot cheese.

"I guess I did kind of miss out on a lot senior year. Fuck, I wish I could go back in time. I would have done it so differently."

"You didn't miss out on everything, don't beat yourself up." She was sidetracked by a text on her phone.

"Who's that?" I slurred.

"Eh, no one important. So, where are you going next on your tour of the friend group?"

"I think I'm going to Colorado to visit Sabrina. She said I can stay with her for a few days. Weed is legal, which is a plus, and she said we can go see a concert at Red Rocks. I've always wanted to do that."

"I love that you're doing this, Brett. Forget Orlando for a while. Nothing good is there for you right now."

She was mostly right. I hadn't seen Luke since he strutted off with that tall goddess of a woman, Gita, at Lana and Tom's party. Lana told me in passing one night that they were dating. Good for them, I thought. They'd make beautiful babies who would probably break a lot of hearts. I was challenging myself to take the high road when it came to people hurting me. I wished Kurt well, too. He clearly couldn't figure out what he wanted in life and that was no longer my job to worry about.

My next stop was Denver, Colorado to see Sabrina. Sabrina was the truly natural beauty of our group: tall, blonde, hysterically funny and the kindest human being on the planet. I had only been to Colorado once when I was a kid. This trip was quite a different experience. Sabrina took me to three different dispensaries all within a block of her house. I tried everything THC-infused. They had candies, cookies and, what I feel is truly God's gift to this earth, THC root beer. After downing one, I pledged to be their spokesperson as I ate an entire family-sized bag of salt and vinegar potato chips.

Then, on my last night, we saw an old rock band from the 90's at Red Rocks. I may have ingested my fair share of edibles but what I experienced that night was ethereal. I have never felt more in awe of the symbiotic relationship between humanity and nature. The performers were sending their voices out among the rocks to be reverberated and ricocheted with the strength of millions of years of formation. We made friends with everyone around us. I stared at the unencumbered night sky for what felt like hours. Sabrina turned to me at the end of the night and asked what I wanted in life. I responded that, for once, I could admit that I had no idea, and that I was okay with it.

My next flight brought me to Austin, Texas. Tara was there, and she was my little artist.

An English major like myself, she was my randomly assigned room-mate when we arrived freshman year at Florida State University. We fell in love instantly and there were many nights that we would turn down going out just to listen to alternative music while we ripped up old t-shirts. I think of her any time I hear Lana Del Rey.

Spending time with Tara in Austin was like an emotional reset. She was as calm as a quiet lake in autumn, yet deep as a boundless ocean. We spent most of my time there painting, out on her back porch drinking wine and recounting our experiences together when we studied abroad in London our junior year. How much fun we had back then. No boyfriends. Just us, wandering roads that had existed for hundreds of years. One night after leaving a bar, Tara told me that I deserved the love that we read about in Shakespeare. She shares the same birthday as my mother. Being with her made me feel the same kind of childlike comfort.

Finally, my last stop brought me to Cleveland, Ohio. Two of my college friends had found themselves there after graduation. Ophelia, whom we called Ophie, was born there and always regretted how her family had uprooted her to the humid continual summer days of Florida. She moved back north the moment she was accepted to law school there. She was incredibly smart, but the type of person who never gave herself enough credit. She constantly joked about her inadequacy to cover-up her insecurities. Ophie was a force who had yet to understand her strength. She could argue her point with facts and hold her ground like no one I'd ever met. As soon as I found out she wanted to be a lawyer, I gave her a dollar and told her she was on retainer for whenever I inevitably fucked up in life.

Karley moved there with her. These two had always been close, and I knew that Karley wanted a change of scenery. Karley was a lot like Ophie in that she never truly saw her worth like the rest of us did. She was beautiful, with dark hair and eyes and perfectly tanned skin year-round. Every guy she was introduced to instantly fell in love with her. But she always frustrated me because she settled for men who treated her like she was expendable. And she wasn't—she was the kind of girl that men would move mountains for. I told her so, one night after too many cheap beers in downtown Cleveland. I asked her to promise me that she wouldn't settle for any more bullshit. Ophie agreed to vet her potential matches a bit more carefully from now on. I was only in Cleveland for two days, but in that amount of time I shared some of the deepest and most honest conversations of my life.

On my final flight home, I sat in my economy-sized seat and went through my purse. It was filled to the brim with tokens from my self-worth journey. Ticket stubs from concerts, beer cozies from local bars, a pair of socks that I had tie-dyed. I considered my next steps. I had just adventured more in the past three weeks than I had in the past five years. I had tried oysters for the first time. I had laughed on the couch with friends until four in the morning. I went out to bars and didn't worry about spending the night alone. This, this was what I had been missing. The self-discovery that comes with challenge. As the flight landed, I was filled with hope. I hadn't felt the need to take more than my prescribed amount of clonazepam the entire trip. I hadn't had one panic attack. I was healing, really healing, from the inside.

As my taxi pulled up to my house in Orlando, I took a deep breath. The idea of walking in there alone no longer felt like a miserable task. I may have been partially to blame for my unhappiness before, but I no longer punished myself with that burden. I would no longer act as Atlas and carry the weight of the world on my shoulders. I shrugged it all off as I placed the key in the lock of the front door.

CHAPTER 13

I walked into the next work week feeling hungry. I wanted to be a junior publisher and I had prepped all week for Thursday's interview. As I stepped into Cheryl's office, I felt unstoppable. I sat down in the chair in front of her and crossed my legs, right over left. Fixing my jacket, I rested my back against the black leather seat. Cheryl leaned forward in her armchair and began.

"Okay. So, how was your trip?" she asked while searching through her laptop inbox.

"It was, for lack of a better word, eye-opening. I can't remember the last time I did soul-searching like that. I feel ready to focus on what's important in my life and, Cheryl, it's this job."

"Wow, well, it's good to see you so sure of yourself. For a while there you seemed...distracted." She looked up momentarily to gauge my reaction.

"Absolutely. I mean, I'm twenty-six and finally in a head space where I feel ready to come into my full potential. No more distractions. This is all that I want." And I meant it.

"That's great to hear because I think you'd make a great fit as junior publisher. Now, it's going to be more work. Some nights you'll be up late with new projects from potential clients. And it's a lot more responsibility... you'll be making more decisions without anyone's guidance. But I think you're ready. What do you say?" With that question she closed her laptop and stared at me, searching for hesitation.

"Yes! I can handle it, I won't let you down." I said. I wouldn't.

"Perfect. I have a new short story author I'd like you to vet. She seems to be a mix of Pynchon and Perkins-Gillman. Interesting and dark. I'll have it on your desk within the hour."

So just like that, the job was mine. I felt my heart skip a beat. I did it. I couldn't believe it.

"By the way, have you got any tampons? My time of the month hit a lot more quickly than it usually does and the bathroom supply is out."

"Let me check my purse," I said, grabbing my purse from the floor, "I actually get it in the beginning of the month, so I shouldn't have any. I'll check."

But as I opened the little secret pouch in my purse where I stored my tampons, it spilled out with the familiar plastic sheaths. They should be gone, I thought. I don't even fill it back up until my next period is nearing, at first tell-tale sign of a piss-y mood and breast tenderness. And then it hit me: I didn't get my period earlier this month.

I never got my period at all.

"Um, Cheryl, I actually can run to the corner store to get you some."

"Are you sure? I can ask around..."

"Nope! No problem, I need them anyways."

It was a lie, but I couldn't tell her why I really needed to go. I needed a pregnancy test. Am I fucking *pregnant*? I felt my heart racing and my chest became tight. Pull it together, I told myself. It's probably just late because I was doing all that blow and not exactly filling my body with nutrients for a while. Forgoing most meals for shots of whiskey will do that to a woman. It throws off the cycle. Right? But I had been cleaning up my act. No more coke, no more shots. I'd eaten so much on my travels. I'd gained a few pounds, even. This didn't make sense. I calmly walked out of Cheryl's office, down the stairs and out the front door of the building. I was walking as fast as my legs could carry me. I said the Lord's Prayer the entire walk to the pharmacy. You can take the girl out of Catholic school. I guess Kurt's mom was getting her way in the end: I was turning towards Jesus for salvation.

As I walked into the drugstore, I sharply turned down the aisle for "family planning." I stumbled upon the pregnancy tests. There were so many options. They all looked the same. I found one that told you "five days sooner" if your life was about to go up in flames. I had never wished more in my life that I needed tampons, as I pulled the box of tests from the shelf. I quickly walked straight to the cashier and paid in cash. As I passed her the bills, she looked at my hand, saw no ring, and looked up into my face with pity. I knew she meant well, but all I wanted to do was punch her in that moment. Don't pity me, lady, I did this to myself. I'm just an idiot.

I rushed to the bathroom of the pharmacy. I didn't want to waste another minute walking back to the office so I could take the test in the well-lit bathroom with its vanity mirror. The dirty stall of a pharmacy bathroom would have to do. As I ripped open the outer box, I stared at the cardboard packaging. So delightful and pink. Charming, even. And the picture of the woman on the front. She looks so happy, I thought, cradling the child to her chest. I pulled out one of the tests and removed the plastic outer shell. It was the size of a small bundle of pencils, but it held the power to change my life forever. I popped off the cap and sat on the toilet. Ten seconds of stream finished. I put the cap back on and let it lay level on the back of the off-white porcelain toilet. And so began the longest three minutes of my entire life.

The entire time I waited, I stared into the mirror above the sink. How could you be so stupid, I demanded of the woman in the reflection? You just let any man inside of you the second he whispers pretty little nothings in your ear. You fucking *idiot*, Brett. You did this. You ruined your life over a man who is in love with someone else. Finally, I looked back towards the toilet to my left. The little rectangle lay there against the white ceramic. Two blue lines, clear as day.

I was pregnant.
Pregnant.

I can't say for sure how long I stayed in that drugstore bathroom. Minutes, maybe hours passed. Finally, I checked my phone to see the time. I had a missed call from Cheryl. I called her back.

"Hey, are you okay? You've been gone for a while, I was worried. Did you take a long lunch?"

"Hey, yeah, I'm sorry. My, um… cramps are killing me," I said hoping she hadn't realized that I said I was nowhere near my time of the month, "Mind if I head home for the day? I'm so sorry."

"No, it's fine. Trust me, I get it. I'll see you tomorrow morning. Congratulations on the promotion, Brett. You earned it."

The promotion.

I hung up the phone. Fuck, the promotion. Would it matter that I'm now pregnant? Am I going to…stay pregnant? Am I having this baby? A million questions that I never wanted to have to answer. Everything came crashing around me. The walls of the bathroom stall moved sideways, and I felt like I was standing on a moving raft in the middle of an ocean. A panic attack.

I searched my purse for the pills. They'd almost become strangers lately; everything had been going so well. Of course, that never lasted, I reminded myself. As my fingers wrapped around the plastic cap, I breathed a small sigh of relief. My whole world may be just about to plummet, but at least I have my clonazepam. I pulled out the medicine bottle and quickly unhinged its lid. I freed two little pills from their vessel. Before capping it, I tipped the bottle ever so slightly once more. Another pill was released.

Without giving it another thought, I threw all three tiny, yellow pills to the back of my throat. I didn't have a water, so I forced myself to dry swallow the little discs. They scraped my esophagus the entire way down. Good, I thought. It should hurt. A little reminder of how much I deserve to be punished for this. I capped the bottle and stood up. Giving myself a last-minute glimpse in the mirror, I noticed something. I couldn't say that I was looking at a stranger this time. I saw myself for who I was in that exact moment: a scared young woman. The mirror couldn't lie to me and tell me everything would be okay. Not even a few clonazepam could make me feel better.

~

I walked into my little home around 6 p.m. that night. After leaving the pharmacy with the knowledge that my uterus was currently housing a factory of splitting cells, I wandered the city for a few hours. I was racking my brain, nervously considering the answer to the hardest question I'd ever had to ask myself: what do I do? I knew that I had to make my decision quickly. With every moment that passed, the awareness that I was actively growing a child inside of myself became more uncomfortable. Unbearable. I wanted children. I had wanted them since I was a child, myself. And, for years, I had wanted a child with Kurt.

Kurt, you *asshole*.

Now, in this moment, a twisted sense of destiny had delivered my dream unto me. However, in a very tragic Shakespearean way, I was fated to actualize this fantasy by myself. And that was what kept resounding in my head like a shriek reverberated over and over again off the walls of a massive canyon: he doesn't want a life with you, Brett. And what is a child, but the most connecting form of relationship two humans can have. If Kurt were to find out about this pregnancy, he would say one of two things. He would either say, "I'll help support the child, but I don't want to be together," or, "I don't want to have a child, we need to have an abortion." Either way, I am on my own.

On my own.

Yes, the baby would have a father if Kurt decided he would be in its life. But that was a giant "if" and Kurt hadn't exactly been a beacon of consistency lately. He didn't know what he wanted, and he was so lost. I couldn't imagine how much more stress and confusion this would add. I just couldn't do it. I couldn't call him up and tell him about all of this. He had stayed with me for so long because I was comfortable for him, I still had no idea when he stopped loving me. I mean, shit, I don't know if he *ever* loved me. Kurt had always given into what I wanted from us and I still didn't know why. I couldn't imagine bringing a child into this world because he thought he wanted it, only to discover he didn't when the baby was in my arms. He'd left me before our wedding day and that hurt. But if he left me with a newborn baby, it would be unendurable. I couldn't do this alone. And so, in that moment, I made my decision. The most selfish thing I had ever done. I was going to have an abortion, and Kurt would never know that I had been pregnant with his child.

CHAPTER 14

There's a strange emotion that pulls up from the deepest parts of your being after you make an entirely selfish decision. It isn't necessarily contentment: in no way was I pleased with myself. It's more like a notion that you've resolved to consider yourself above all else, and that you feel validated. That is, as long as you can convince yourself that it's what is best for everyone, even if they may not see it.

I began doing that immediately with my decision to have an abortion. I wasn't changing my mind; I couldn't tell Kurt and risk him telling me I was making a mistake. I knew that even if he told me he would help me raise the baby, even if he said he would stand by me – there was absolutely no way that I could believe him. He had let me down time and time again. Even if he meant well and resolved to stay with me, it wouldn't last. It never did. So, I started the process no woman ever wishes to begin. I looked online for abortion clinics in my city.

I want to make something very clear: I despised myself for this. As I scoured the internet for the best rated clinics in Orlando, I continuously screamed hateful words to my conscious. I called myself an idiot, I called myself selfish and evil. I reprimanded myself for being so wrapped up in the false pretense of Kurt's touch that I neglected responsibility. The one thing I wouldn't let myself really feel was the realization that my body was home to the beginnings of a child. Our child. Cells were separating, connections were being made. The thought of it made me sick. Not because I didn't want children. I really had always wanted a baby. Babies. Even more painful, I wanted a baby with Kurt. But this wasn't the way it was supposed to happen. We were supposed to be together, in love, trying for a baby. And now, I was alone. I was looking for a place to steal the child from my womb, when I should have been curled into Kurt's arms, searching for maternity wear, together.

I felt sick. I ran to the bathroom and sat in front of the toilet. Nothing felt real. It was as if I were floating above myself, watching myself dry heave into a sparkling, ceramic bowl. I knew I couldn't hold on to this alone any longer. I couldn't tell my parents. I knew that they wouldn't disprove, necessarily. They'd realize that I was alone and that, above all else, I just wasn't ready. Although they'd sent me to Catholic school my entire life, it wasn't for the religious upbringing so much as a stellar education. Public schools in Orlando weren't exactly the greatest in the early 90s. Though they were also raised in Catholic households, they weren't religious in any traditional sense and loved me more than any doctrine, no matter how deeply inlaid. It was a painful thought because they would be so sad for me. Any pain I went through, they felt ten-fold.

It had always been this way.

As I typed in my mother's cell phone number, I paused for a moment. I recalled when I had to have a cyst aspirated in my breast when I was sixteen. It wasn't cancerous, but it could have been had it been left to simmer. So, a doctor numbed my left breast, and sent a massive, hollow needle through the skin and the fat of it in order to reach the mass. The invader. Though they may have used a numbing agent on the area, I still felt the awful, agonizing pressure of an object penetrating my body. I looked over at my mother who stayed in the room for emotional support. I needed her to portray a calm demeanor, to tell me everything was okay, to ask me to just stay strong and that it would be over soon. Instead, I found her weeping. She was crying because her little girl was in pain, and that devastated her just as much as it did me. She had such a massive heart, and it destroyed her to see me suffering. She was such a natural mother.

Remembering all of this, I deleted her number from my keypad. I couldn't put them through this.

It would only add to the pain I was already feeling.

I was still aware that there was no way I could do this alone. It was too much for any woman to experience isolated. It wasn't the pain I was worried about, although I had to admit I had no idea what to expect. I was more worried about the shock of undergoing what felt like a very mature, or immature, decision depending on how you looked at it. I was choosing to end a potential life. This wasn't something that you do without something, someone to lean on. Even if I felt like I didn't deserve that support. I just needed someone who loved me enough to not judge me for this. Someone who would be strong enough to stay focused on making this process easier.

Phoebe. I needed Phoebe.

Quickly, I pulled her number up from my contacts. It wasn't hard to find it; I had called her nearly daily for the past few months. Phoebe never ceased to amaze me with her ability to drop everything to ensure that I was surviving. Again, she picked up after one ring.

"Hey, Brett! How did the interview go? Tell me you got the job and we have a reason to celebrate this weekend."

"Um, yeah, I actually got the job," I said with zero emotion.

"Oh, my god! Congrats, man! Why do you sound like someone ran over your cat, then?

The most depressed way to say good news I've ever heard."

"Because, Pheebs, I'm fucking pregnant."

I didn't hear her speak for about ten seconds.

"You're, hold on. You're pregnant? When, how? Whose is it, Brett?"

"I mean, it's Kurt's. I haven't slept with anyone else and I used a condom with Luke. I'm a fucking idiot – I had... last month. He came over and... it was just once. We didn't use a condom."

Again.
Silence.
Was she mad that I had gone back to him?
Disappointed?

"Okay. Okay, um, okay. *Shit*, sorry I just, what did he say when you told him?"

"I didn't tell him. I'm not going to tell him." I was firm in this decision. This wasn't open for debate.

"What do you mean, Brett? Are you *still* seeing him? You can't not tell him that you're having his child. How are you going to keep that from him?"

"I mean, it'll be easy. I'm not keeping it."

Another few seconds of silence passed between us.
They felt like ten minutes.

"Okay. Whatever you decide, I've got your back. You know that. What's the plan, then?"

"Well, I only found out yesterday," I said, "but I'm not going to lie to you, knowing that I have this... just, knowing that this is happening inside my body, every second has been torture. I can't wait any longer. I can't just... I need to do this fast. I found a place here in town. I'm making an appointment for Friday."

"Okay, I'll be there. I would come there tonight but I need to finish this project for work.

I can see if I can push it to Monday."

"No, Pheebs, don't worry about it. Listen, I can go over to Lana and Tom's tonight. Just, thank you. You have no idea what it means to me to know that you'll be there with me. I can't do this alone." I felt myself tearing up. Pull it together, I demanded.

"Absolutely. One hundred percent, you know I'm there. And, Brett, you're sure you don't want to tell Kurt....?" Her voice trailed off.

"No, no fucking way. He's done enough already. What if he tries to tell me to keep it? I can't... Pheebs, I couldn't survive that. I can't trust that he'd stay. I already decided what I'm going to do. I'm not changing my mind and I'm sure as hell not waiting another day. I'll be fine, I'll see you tomorrow, okay? I won't be alone tonight; I'll be with friends."

"Okay, Brett. I love you; you are *not* alone in this."

And with that promise, I hung up and called the clinic. Within minutes, I had an appointment set for Friday, tomorrow. The woman on the phone was so robotic, it unnerved me. I assumed that, yes, she had done this plenty of times. Talked a woman through the process. She informed me that I would come in for my initial appointment at 4 p.m.

Whenever we had to have "life skills" sessions in religion class, they made a point to make the idea of having sex before marriage a truly terrifying and risky experience. We were made to create presentations about STIs and unplanned pregnancies complemented with large poster visuals of outbreaks and abortions. Threats of hell to these horrible sinners. I remember how large everyone's eyes were as they took all this information in, hearing the whispers of fourteen-year-old girls saying, "How could a girl be so awful as to destroy a baby like that?" Computer-pixelated images of bloodied tiny body parts ripped from the safety of their young mother's wombs. In that moment, I silently swore to myself that, no matter what, I would never be a monster and kill my own baby. I wouldn't be so selfish, so immoral. And here I was, about ten years later, signing my soul to the devil. I thanked the woman at the clinic, informed her that I would be having the medical abortion and ended the call.

The minutes after I ended that call, I sat in surreal silence. I couldn't believe that this was happening. I just found out that I was pregnant and already I was less than 24 hours from ending it. The speed of setting up this appointment, the ease of making this problem go away – it made me nauseous. I hadn't even taken a moment to breathe, let alone consider the effects of it all. I took a moment to place my right hand on my abdomen, just below my belly button. I thought, what if I didn't do this? I could call Kurt. Maybe he would be happy. And, in just nine months, we would have a child. Or maybe it was ten months? I had heard that somewhere. What would my life look like then?

Lonely. Kurt was too lost to consider a family with me. The queasiness I felt at the thought of going through with it made me pull my hand away from my gut like it had been placed on a hot stove. I needed Friday to come. I needed to forget this feeling of housing a human being, knowing that it was ever so slowly growing, only to be ripped out and destroyed at the source. I hated myself so much for being so self-centered, so greedy as to think that my happiness was bigger than anyone else's. I needed to forget.

Quickly, I called Lana. She didn't answer, which was odd. She always had her phone with her. I texted Tom to see what they were doing that night. I needed to be with people. Phoebe wouldn't be here until tomorrow for the appointment, and I couldn't be alone until then. My hand wandered to my stomach once more.

Me:

> Hey, I tried Lana, but she didn't answer.
> Y'all got plans tonight?

Tom:

> Hey, stranger!
> Yeah, she's out at a friend's place
> but should be home later.
> Come on over,
> I want to hear all about your adventures.

Me:

> Thanks, Tom.
> I just need to drink.
> Shit's not great right now.
> I'll be over soon.

Tom:

> I'll have your whiskey waiting, my dear.

He was no Phoebe, but in the past couple of months he had become like a brother to me. Tom had a lightness to him, he made those around him laugh while always seeming to get people into such deep conversations. A few weeks ago, at a happy hour at our favorite Asian bar, he and a few friends had started the night with sake bombs. Quickly, it turned into a wild round of their favorite bar game, "Dare or Dare." The rules were as simple as they sounded – you may only pick dare and must complete whatever task is dealt. If you don't, you can never play again. As you can imagine, playing this game in a public restaurant can develop into quite the wild round. On this particular evening, Tom ended up watering all the fake plants in the place, even the ones at people's tables. Within a few minutes of this, we were all escorted off the property and threatened with a ban. Lana was fuming. It put a black mark on her reputation. I had never laughed so hard in my life. Next time we showed up at that restaurant, there was a friendly paper reminder placed on the tables that the plants were, indeed, fake and did not need watering by patrons.

Thinking back on this memory, I changed out of my work clothes and into sweatpants and a t-shirt. I wasn't dressing up for anything: we weren't going out and I had no desire to. I think that even if I had tried to look relatively human, no makeup would have been able to cover up the pain I was feeling. I tried to look in the mirror quickly before I headed out the door, just to ensure that I didn't look as terrible as I felt. It was a mistake. Even taking a moment to see my reflection made me feel sick. I knew in that moment that it would be a while before I could face myself again. I would tuck the painting away to rot elsewhere.

I needed to take the edge off, and even the ten-minute drive to Tom and Lana's was too much time without something in my system. I walked over to the kitchen and pulled the bottle of Jameson from the shelf above the fridge. My liquor cabinet was nothing impressive, but it did contain the largest bottle of whiskey I had ever seen. I brought a shot glass down from that same shelf. I poured the whiskey in it and watched it fill with the thick, brown liquid. Without considering it another moment, I threw it back towards the back of my throat. It didn't go down easy, the sharp flavour hit my insides in a way that made me want to instantly send it back up from where it came. I was still too worked up to allow my body to settle. I needed another couple of shots to force it to do so. I needed to feel numb. Two more shots and I was ready to go.

Placing myself in my car, I sat for a minute with the keys in my hand. I was already three shots in, and there was no way I would be able to drive later. Weighing my decision to avoid a potential disaster, I thought – who cares? If I ended up in a drunk-driving accident, then maybe it would solve my problem. "Fuck, snap out of it," I told myself. I pulled the keys back out of the ignition. I was not that far gone, I lied to myself. Things would get better. Another lie, but this I still believed, even if it was just a small amount.

I slid the keys back into the ignition and pulled out of the driveway.

CHAPTER 15

walked into Tom and Lana's apartment feeling woozy. Maybe it was the three shots I took within a minute. Maybe it was the burden of tomorrow's decision weighing on me. Whatever it was, I felt as though every step I took was a struggle, as if at any moment I may just crumple upon the floor into a mess of pure chaos. Tom called me to the couch.

"Hey, dude," he said happily, "Woah, you, uh.. okay? You look—"

"Terrible. I'm aware."

He looked me up and down, trying to assess the damage. He couldn't find any obvious injury, so he just waited, calmly, for me to self-diagnose.

"I've had a hell of a couple days. I just need to get hammered. Lana not home yet?"

"Alright, well, we can achieve that easily. Lana is actually out for the night. Apparently, her sorority sisters are dragging her into a full night of karaoke and social climbing. God, I wish she'd never joined sometimes." He looked genuinely angry.

"I can imagine. But has she ever shown any... different side to her? She's always kind of struck me as the 'Greek-life' type." I was drunk and prying.

"Sure, she's beautiful and outgoing," he said as he poured four shots, "but I always thought she was unique, you know? She marched to the beat of her own drum. Now, she's a carbon copy of her conceited fucking 'big.'"

To be honest, Lana had never seemed to me as anything other than a sorority girl. I'd spent a few nights with her and her friends. It wasn't exactly what I would call enjoyable. She dressed like her "sisters," she talked like them and she even fed on gossip like they did. I really only knew a few girls like that in college and to me, she was a dead ringer. I couldn't understand how Tom was so shocked by this descension into Stepford Wifedom. But he appeared to be dealing with a major reality check, and I wanted to help him work through it. It was the least I could do to thank him for his kindness over the months. We downed all four shots – two each, back to back.

The room rocked ever so slightly.

"Look," I said wiping my lip to catch the whiskey dribble, "if you love her, that's all that matters, right? I mean, you can't change someone. Trust me, you can't. But if she genuinely has turned into a person you no longer see yourself with, then that's a different story."

"I think I just always imagined that we'd grow together. I knew she was younger, but that never really showed itself, you know? She was always such a fucking go-getter. I loved that about her. She wanted to be the next Hillary Clinton. Now, all she does is redecorate our apartment and read Good Housekeeping. If she walks in here with one more 'Live, Laugh, Love' sign I'm going to lose it."

At that confession, we both started laughing hysterically. It was true, the house was covered in that maddening slogan. Everywhere we looked, we pointed another one out to each other and started giggling again. I didn't know if it was the whiskey-ridden joke or the fact that my life was a mess, but I had begun laughing so hard I was near tears. By the time he pointed out the "Home is Where the Martinis Are" framed picture, I had begun bawling. Tom moved closer to me and put his arm around my shoulder.

"Brett, I know you don't really want to talk about it, but you have to tell me what's going on. Please." His expression was one of pure concern.

"Fuck, Tom, I don't even know where to start. Honestly, it's fucking Kurt, okay? He just... God! He fucked me up."

"What do you mean? What did he do?"

I felt his breath near my face.
It smelled like whiskey and weed.
Too much like Kurt's.
I stood up and walked across the room.
I needed to move.

"He just, he ruined me. He broke up with me right before our wedding. He fell in love with some other fucking probably *perfect* girl who he never even had the *decency* to tell me who it was. I think about this girl all the fucking time, Tom. Seriously, every *god damn* day I try to picture her. It haunts me. *She* does. And then he—"

I couldn't finish the sentence. My vision was a blurry mess and my head was swimming in whiskey waters. I crumbled to the floor like a marionette who lost her strings. Remembering I was currently poisoning the child growing inside of me, I felt so guilty. The fact that I was going to be aborting it tomorrow made me feel sick. Tom poured another couple of shots and I grabbed another one off of the table and threw it back through tears. The world around me started to melt away. Tom moved to the floor and put his arm around me, leading me to the couch. I sat next to him and cried harder than I have in my entire life. Then, everything went black.

~

I woke up with my head on his lap. I'm not sure when I fell asleep, I don't remember anything after the broken damn of bitter tears. I didn't stir, I didn't move. My eyes were open, but I couldn't move.

Tom had his hand under my shirt.

Slowly, he was tracing the edges of my nipple, and he was whispering.

He thought I was still asleep.
How long had he been doing this before I woke up?

His finger angrily flicked my nipple,
and he moved his hand to cup my entire breast,
squeezing it.
I was frozen.
I didn't know what to do.

He moved his hand down my ribs and to my waist.
His hands were rough and foreign.
Unwanted.
I felt sick.
I wanted to run.
But I was scared.
What if he tried to do more?

He moved his hands down to my pants
and tried to place his hands inside,
when –

Keys jangled in the lock of the apartment door. I sprang up as he moved away from me. I didn't turn to meet his gaze. I never wanted to look him in the eyes again. All I wanted was to get as far away from this couch as possible. I stared at the front door. Lana walked into the apartment. Upon seeing us on the couch together, she made an inadvertent frown. She held it as she looked at me and then placed her gaze, fiery and angry, upon Tom. I had never seen her maintain anything for more than a few seconds other than a smile.

Quickly, I grabbed my purse from the floor, placed the sleeve of my shirt back up off of my arm and onto my shoulder, and moved to leave. Lana stayed perfectly still by the door, unmoving. As I hurriedly approached her on my way to the door, she kept her eyes on Tom. Finally, as I walked past her, she looked at me, dead in the eyes. I expected to see anger, but all I saw was embarrassment. Her eyes were almost apologetic. Confused, I looked down and ran out the door into the hallway.

As I raced to my car, my feet were moving without my instruction. They were unfamiliar to me. Their gait, quick and frantic, was not mine. They were entirely severed from me in that moment. Every piece of my body felt alien to me. As I approached my car I raised my right hand to unlock the driver's side door. It was shaking so badly, I couldn't steady it enough to fit the key into the lock. As I desperately asked my hand to calm itself again, I felt that I was demanding something of a stranger's hand. And how could I command someone else's body to do anything for me?

Finally, after too many attempts to count, the key slid into the lock, and with a jerk of the wrist, the car was unlocked. I fell inside, awkwardly, and was still. I couldn't bring my arm, this stranger's limb, to put the keys in the ignition. So, I sat in the car and I waited.

I waited to cry.
I waited to scream.

But I couldn't.
Nothing came.

I merely sat, dull-eyed and numb.

~

At some point, my arm must have obeyed. The next thing I knew, I was sitting in my driveway, and I was home. To be honest, I couldn't explain how I had gotten there. Yes, I was drunk. I knew that, objectively, that was the wrong thing to have done tonight. To be honest, I didn't care. I'm not saying that I weighed the options as I sat in the car in the parking lot of Tom's and Lana's apartment. I didn't consider the benefits of doing the responsible thing for myself and everyone else and contemplate calling an Uber. I didn't, then, take a self-assessment in the moment and decide that I was sober enough to drive. I had just driven because my body knew that was what you do when you're sitting in a driver's seat of a car, alone. Autopilot, I've heard it called.

CHAPTER 16

At some point that night, I must have left the car and gone inside the house. I woke up the next morning, fully dressed in the clothes from the night before, in a small ball on top of the bed. I hadn't even slid my body under the covers. I checked my phone. It was 1 p.m. and I had no sense of what time I returned home last night. I had no idea what time I had awoken to the hands of a man I thought was my friend on my body. Feeling me. At the thought of that, I felt sick. I wanted to pull myself out of my own skin and sterilize it. I needed to cleanse myself of the entire night, inside and out. But that would be impossible, I reminded myself. That night won't be going anywhere. All I could do was take a scalding-hot shower and move on with my day. And how easy that was going to be, I almost laughed to myself at the realization. Today was the day I would abort my first child.

On my way to the bathroom, I momentarily caught my reflection in my mirror. I had stared into it so many times before. Light and dark days, sad and happy moments, all captured. Looking into my eyes, for the first time I felt jealousy for my reflection. It was so one-dimensional. The existence of my reflection was an easy one, merely mimicking the original Brett. My painting. My reflection had no experiences other than the one I gave it. It didn't have to suffer through anything other than what I showed it. Proving that point, I twisted my face into a smile. Painful and sharply false, the image of my face contorted in such an emotion was frightening. Did it seem slower to mimic me? Like it was lagging? I allowed my cheeks to fall, to settle into its natural state. Not quite a frown: a frown would imply an emotion, even if a negative one. My face fell into nothing, and nothing will come of nothing.

Suddenly, I was aware of my clothes. I looked down and saw that I was wearing my outfit from last night.

Last night.

The realization left me feeling an all-encompassing queasiness. I tore at my shirt like an animal. Pulling and ripping, I peeled it off of my skin and onto the floor. In one fell swoop, I tugged my pants over my feet. I kicked the clothes under the bed and out of my sight. I didn't look in the mirror again. I just ran, ashamed, into the shower.

Was it somehow my fault?

I didn't take any time to test the temperature of the water before I threw my body into the light rain. It wasn't hot, but I didn't care. All that mattered was that I was getting clean. I leaned my body against the cool off-white tiles of the shower walls. Slowly, I let my body fall. It slid down to the floor and landed with a thud. It may have been hard enough to cause a bruise, but my mouth didn't let out a sound. I just sat there, in the luke-warm comfort of cleansing droplets. Each one that fell on my skin was an apology. But it was too late for that. I may have cried, but I couldn't say for sure. The water hid and forgave that shameful honesty.

~

The next thing I knew, I was getting a phone call. I didn't know how long I'd been in the shower, but it was long enough for the water to pierce my skin with its ice-cold droplets. I pulled the towel I'd left on the floor around myself, tightly and securely. As I shuffled on damp feet to the nightstand and my phone, I saw that it was Phoebe trying to call me. Before I dialed her number, I noticed that my mother had sent me a video. I opened it and saw that she and my father had recorded it in front of her favorite birdfeeder in their garden. Gracefully placed inside it was a red cardinal – her favorite bird of them all. It was delicately feeding on seeds while my parents narrated the event in awe.

"Look, Brett, look who is stopping by to say 'Hello!'" my mother said excitedly.

"Brett, your mother thinks this is the same one as last week. Either it is and we have a new pet, or she's going crazy and thinks it's her dead aunt visiting her from beyond the grave. Either way—help," my dad said, amidst my mother's beautiful laughs.

The video ended with my dad smiling at the camera and my mother turned, mid-laughter, towards him.

They were so happy.

In that moment, I resolved: I couldn't tell them about last night.
I would never tell anyone.

I wrote up a message on my phone in one fluid movement. I didn't consider it or edit one word. Without thinking any further, I sent it to Tom. It said:

Me:

You know what you fucking did last night
was beyond unacceptable.
You sexually assaulted me when I was asleep.
I woke up.
How could you?
I thought you were my friend.

You knew I was going through something
and you fucking took advantage of me
when I was in a dark moment.
If you ever tell anyone anything other than
what really happened,
I will call my cousin who is a lawyer
and send you to jail.

You're a goddamn piece of shit
and the only reason I'm not
bringing you to court right this second
is because I don't want to relive
that moment ever again.

Speak a word and I'm telling Lana
and the authorities everything.
Do not write me back –
I never want to hear from you ever again.
We are not friends.

If I had told anyone what happened, I'm sure they would have told me that I didn't handle this properly. They would have told me to call the cops and have him arrested for sexual assault. They would have told me to take him to court and tell a jury of my peers what he did to me and ask them to lock him away. But they had no idea how this process really goes.

Women are seldom believed. It's nearly impossible to lock someone away for rape let alone sexual assault.

I'd have to go on the stand and describe what happened to me in front of dozens of people who would be eyeing me up and down, checking for inconsistencies. They would scour my records and social media, finding pictures that they would deem "trampy" or "asking for it." They would find flirty posts left on friends' walls and call me "easy." Rape is the only crime where the victim has to prove the deed has been done. And they would say that I wasn't even raped, so where is the crime? I was drunk and had brought myself to a man's house alone, so where's the crime? God, they could even find proof that I had an abortion scheduled for the next day and use that against me. Everyone would know every detail of my personal life. If I sued, I wouldn't win. All that would happen: another woman burned at the stake. There really was no point, I couldn't do anything.

I deleted my outgoing message to Tom and with it, the entire event. I would ignore it as if it never happened. I would bury it deep, deep down where no one would ever find it. Hopefully, one day, even I would forget it resided there.

Forget.

I checked the phone: 3 p.m. on the dot. I needed to be at the clinic at 4 p.m. I called Phoebe.

"Hey, Brett. How are you feeling? I know today must be really hard to imagine going through…," she said, her voice trailing off.

"Honestly, I'm fine," I lied, "I'm just ready for this to be over. How far away are you?"

"Less than twenty. What did you do last night?"

Flashes.

Fingers irritably grabbing at me.

Slow, uncomfortable nails dragging against my skin.

My heart beating out of my chest.

Silently begging to be anywhere else but there.

"Nothing. Just text me when you're outside. The place is about fifteen minutes away, so I'll just come out when you get here."

I was being short, but that had nothing to do with her. Last night was steeping in my head. I wished I could just remove the night from my memory, like simply taking out a tea bag that has soaked in a mug for too long, leaving the water dark and bitter. I didn't want to think about anything. Any moment when I was left alone with my thoughts was damaging. I started digging my nails into my thigh just to divert my mind from the inner disorder. The sharp pinch of it quieted my thoughts, even if only mildly and temporarily.

As I waited for Phoebe to text me, I sat in one of the chairs at my kitchen table. I sat in silence. No book was in my hands; my fingers were empty and held no pages. No computer glowed with work plastered across the screen. No music danced across the room, bouncing against the walls and reverberating off of my vacant ear drums. I spent those twenty agonizing minutes in limbo. Partially present but entirely lost. I couldn't wait for this day to be over and to start again tomorrow. At least I had that: the ability to pull myself up and out. I would forget it all ever happened.

As I watched Phoebe pull into my driveway, I felt my stomach turn. I grabbed the biggest sweatshirt I could find and pulled it over my head, feeling myself drown in the fabric. It was raining, but I didn't grab an umbrella.

"Are you okay?" Phoebe asked when she saw me, "I mean, I know you're not. Today is…well…it's going to be hard. How are you feeling?" She always rambled when she was nervous. She was never a good liar.

"I'm fine, Pheebs. Sorry I just… didn't sleep well last night. A lot on my mind, you know? But, seriously, thank you so much for coming with me. I couldn't imagine doing this alone."

Alone.

"Of course, dude. I'm just going to ask you this one more time: are you *sure* that you don't want to tell Kurt about any of this? Don't get mad at me, I just feel like he should know."

"Listen, man, I haven't heard from him since that night. He clearly doesn't give a shit about me and, honestly, if that's the case why should he care about this? No, Pheebs. He's not a part of this. I can handle it myself."

I spit the words out with more venom than I had meant to. I was doing that a lot lately.

"Okay, okay. I just, I'm worried about you. You keep saying you're alone. You're not, Brett. You have your parents who *adore* you. They even text me making sure you're okay when you don't talk to them for a day. And you have so many friends. All of us from college. And you know you're my sister."

"I know, I know. I'm sorry I'm just a little overwhelmed with everything."

"I can imagine. At least you have friends here now! That must be a comfort, to be able to go chill with Lana and Tom when you need a breather."

The thought of being back in that apartment made my skin crawl. I had the sudden urge to rip off the outer layer of my body. I wanted to be like the amphibious creatures in one of Vonnegut's short stories and step out of my body's "clothes." Let my soul drift to find a home in a more comfortable vessel. I couldn't breathe in this outfit.

I noticed that I hadn't been breathing for a while. Shallow, quick breaths had gotten me by until now. But then, my body realized what it had been deprived of. I felt my arms and legs start to tingle. My stomach was cramping, and the blood was rushing from my head. As everything started to turn dark, I made a last-ditch effort to find the clonazepam in my purse. I could see Phoebe watching me from the corner of my eye. Finally, I clasped the pills in my hand, my fingers clenching around the orange, hard, plastic bottle. I had gotten them refilled. So many pills now. As I pried open the lid, I set free two pills into my palm. I threw them back, quick and fluid like a shot, and took a gulp of Phoebe's soda. The satisfaction of knowing that the pills were currently dissolving in my blood stream and would soon slow my body down allowed my breathing to deepen and my vision to refocus.

"Did you just have another one?"

"Yeah, it was bad. My hands started to cramp. I couldn't see."

"I mean, it makes sense. So, don't be too hard on yourself. Today was bound to take its toll in more ways than one," she said. "Did they tell you what to expect when you called?"

"Not exactly," I said as I tried to focus my breathing. "They just said I'll be going through multiple appointments today. A clinical assessment, a sonogram and then the one where the doctor gives me the pills."

"Damn, well, at least they're thorough. Either way, I'll be in the waiting room the whole time. I'm not sure if they'll let me back with you, but you know if they do, I'll be there, too."

I looked over to my left and at the face of my very best friend. She was staring straight ahead at the road but had taken her right hand off of the steering wheel to hold mine. The sun was starting to lower in the afternoon skies and a ray of it skipped across the side of her face. In that moment, she was a goddess to me. I couldn't fathom doing all of this alone. I opened my mouth to tell her about last night. I wanted to share what happened, to have her tell me to do something about it, to swear that she'd fight with me to make Tom pay. But, instead, I closed my mouth.

What was the point in getting her to pick up her weapon, when there was no place to strike it? Instead, we rode in silence, hand in hand like Thelma and Louise, ready for the cliff.

CHAPTER 17

As we sat at a stoplight on Maitland Boulevard, I tried to take survey of how I was feeling. I rattled my mind for some indication of how well or how poorly my psyche was handling all of this. The red light was still blazing ahead of us, longer than usual. Strange, I thought. It was haunting in a way. Commanding everything before it to stop. Part of me wanted the bright, red, all-watching eye to keep its hue. Stay angry, I begged it, I'll listen. But then it quickly disappeared and a vibrant, kelly-green reluctantly appeared in its place. Go, it invited, softly. As we turned left, I rotated my head to follow the traffic light as far as my neck would allow. I wanted to see the red return.

I came back to reality when I heard Phoebe cursing as we neared the clinic. I couldn't believe what I saw. Just like in the movies, there were picketers lining the sidewalk between the parking lot and the front of the office. They were violently stabbing these handmade cardboard signs in the air, all of which were donned with pictures of dissected fetuses and quotes written in black ink.

"Oh, you've got to be fucking kidding me," Phoebe spit out as she pulled the car into the lot.

"Wow. I honestly didn't know that this was a real thing," I said, devoid of emotion.

"Fuck, I'm so sorry," she said mournfully, "that is such bullshit. Don't they have a bible camp they're missing? I mean, Jesus Christ. Fuck these assholes."

"Ironically," I said, "I think they feel they're doing God's work here. Remember, I went to a Catholic school. Our religion class sophomore year revolved around all the reasons someone would go to hell. Trust me when I say that abortion is one of the worst. Man, I swore I would never do something so terrible..."

I lost my train of thought as I found myself again in that memory of being scolded by a woman wearing braces in her fifties. She stood at the front of the schoolroom instructing religion class, one hand on her hip and the other pointing at unnecessarily graphic poster boards made by my classmates. Each one explicitly informed all of us with full-colour images of the guaranteed effects that sex before marriage would cause: painful and isolating STI's, unwanted pregnancy with a terrible mate, or eternal damnation after a murderous abortion of one of God's children. What judgmental, restrictive years. The days when fear governed my choices. The images of that final poster seeped into my brain once again as I felt Phoebe touch my arm.

"Hey, are you okay? Talk to me," she tested.

"Yeah, shit, sorry. Catholic school indoctrination had for me a minute. Count yourself lucky that you didn't have to detox from that as an adult."

"I can't imagine. Look, don't let these idiots make you feel for even a *second* that you're a bad person for this. I don't know what they're going to say when we walk past them, but from what I've seen on TV, they're going to try and make you feel extremely guilty. Do *not* let them, do you hear me?"

She said that last sentence with pure ferocity and conviction. In that moment, I was more nervous of what she was going to do to these bible-thumpers and less so for what was about to happen once I got inside.

"I know, don't worry. I know I'm making the right decision. Just don't, like, fight these guys. I can't bail you out of jail today," I said, nudging her jokingly.

She was nearly vibrating with anger. "Ugh, fine. But they so much as read *one* line of scripture to me and I will throw down."

As we shared one last look, I nodded to her. She pulled the keys out of the ignition and she stepped out of the car. Taking one last shallow breath in, I opened my car door and stepped onto the hot asphalt. Walking up to the sidewalk, I was nearly impressed by the conviction of the picketers. Florida summers are unforgiving, and I was already dripping after ten steps. As we got closer to the mob of Christians, we could smell the sweat. Suddenly, we were within earshot. That's when the insults began.

"Don't kill your child! That is God's angel in your belly!"
"Abortion is *murder!* Hell is waiting for you!"
"God gave you this baby for a reason! You have life inside of you!"

The lineup was actually impressive. We were only about halfway through the onslaught. Bibles were lunged in our faces. Rosaries shook in praying hands. Images of babies torn from their mother's uteruses clouded my vision. I turned to lock eyes with Phoebe. I read her lips, and saw that she was mouthing the words, "Look at me, look at me." That was when I heard a bible verse that brought me back to school masses in my crisp, newly washed, plaid uniform.

"The Lord said: 'Before I formed you in the womb, I knew you, before you were born, I set you apart!' If you do this, you are damned!"

Hearing this, I stopped and turned toward the woman speaking. She wore a long, denim skirt and a crisp, white linen button-down. Before I realized what I was doing, I was channeling a religious part of me that I hadn't visited in years.

"You know what *else* God said!? 'Judge not, that you be not judged'. So, are you *really* the one who should be casting the first stone?! Fuck off!"

For a moment, the crowd of self-righteous were silenced. They had been hit with a taste of their own spiritual medicine. It was always my favorite quote in the Bible for a reason. It typically had the power to make anyone think about how they treated others when they were at their most condemnatory. The moment of quiet didn't last. As we neared the end of the lineup, I heard the onslaught continue. The insults became more heated. Clearly their moment of self-reflection ended in a desire to make me feel hellfire.

"Slut!"
"Heathen!"
"You'll burn!"
"Murderer!"

As we approached the clinic and walked through its doors of both salvation and damnation, their roars faded away. I knew I would never forget that moment, so long as I lived.

Phoebe sat next to me as I filled out the paperwork. The woman who gave me the forms was kind. She smiled to me as she passed me the papers, a mixed expression: one of apology and hope. I appreciated the honesty in her face. I could feel that with each woman she met here, a part of her held on to their pain.

The forms were fairly standard, I imagined, but they were never-ending. I flipped through the pages. Registration forms, medical history, abortion questionnaire, medical abortion care instructions, surgical abortion care instructions, general risks and consent. It was all a bit overwhelming. I read through the questionnaire. It asked if I was nervous, if I wanted to be referred to someone for spiritual support, and how sure I was about my decision. My pen hovered above the answers to that final question, the boxes marked "yes" or "no." I knew my answer, but it felt too final. I told myself I'd do this last. I moved on to the care instructions for both types of abortion procedures. Before arriving, I had already decided on a medical abortion. From what I read online, it was simple: take two pills and it's over. The surgical option seemed so *invasive*, so hostile. I wanted to do this in the comfort of my home, not on a table in a cold room, surrounded by steel in a doctor's office.

Upon reviewing and signing all the documents, I flipped back to the questionnaire and that final question to be answered. Was I sure about my decision? For a moment, I grabbed my cellphone. I was panicking, I wanted to call Kurt. A massive wave of guilt was washing over me, and I felt like I was drowning under its weight. This was his decision to make just as much as it was mine. How could I do this without him? I was about to dial his number when I felt Phoebe watching me. Without looking at her, I scrolled down and away from his contact. I couldn't let her know I was having second thoughts. This was the fruit of a poisonous tree, after all. Luckily, she didn't try and talk me through what she had just seen. She pulled out her own phone and started texting. I was thankful that I didn't have to explain all the crashing thoughts rippling through my mind at that moment. I put my phone away and I made my decision.

I checked a box.

"Yes." I was sure.

It felt like hours had passed between giving the nurse with the kind face my forms, and finally being called back.

"Brett?" a woman called from behind a half-opened door. Phoebe and I stood up and walked to meet her.

"Sorry, honey, only you can come back," she said to me.

Phoebe looked at her, ready to fight back. I grabbed her hand and she turned to meet my eyes.

"It's okay, Pheebs. I'll be fine," I told her.

I had no idea if I meant it. Luckily, she believed me. She squeezed my hand, soft yet firm. Since we had met, we'd done this when saying "goodbye" to each other. One tight squeeze. "I love you." Standing beneath the door frame, we both stood in limbo. She turned away and walked back toward the bright lights of the waiting room. I walked out the other side and approached the dark corridor lined with closed doors.

As we were walking, myself and a shockingly thin nurse, I couldn't help but analyze her figure. She was tall and she moved with purpose, her steps were wide and unwavering. But when she would turn back to ensure that I was following, her face betrayed her resolve. She was tired and dejected. I thought maybe it was because she was merely overworked, and not entirely beaten down by what she saw in this place, day after day. The walk never seemed to end. She was taking me to the furthest room at the very end of the hallway. I was to be tucked away, I thought to myself. Maybe they'd forget I was here; the waiting room was full and there were a shocking number of rooms in the hallway. Easy for someone to go missing this way. But as the nurse led me into my room, numbered twelve, she assured me that someone would be with me momentarily.

As she turned to leave, I asked her what her name was. To this day, I'm not sure why I did that. "Theresa," she told me with a somewhat surprised half-smile. My mother's name. I could tell by her pause before answering that she didn't often get that question here. For whatever reason, giving her a name left me feeling a small sense of calm, no matter how insignificant. She was already out the door before I could tell her mine.

Alone, I studied the room I was in. It was disturbingly monochrome: everything was either brazenly white or plated in silver steel. It was similar to the hospital rooms that I wound up in as a child. I spied the shiny medical instruments on the marble counter, the computer monitor that could tell me in real-time that my vitals were normal and that my body was running smoothly, the Lazy-Boy type lounger covered in clean, crisp paper. But as I began to walk myself to the recliner, I saw the cart tucked into the corner, away from immediate sight. My stomach fell to my knees.

The instruments on that metal sheet were not meant to fix any typical ailment like broken bones or infected bites. It was lined with long scissor-like objects with sharp curves, small vacuums with massive, hollow barrels and stretched syringes used to aspirate. I sat down in the only chair in the room, near the door. I placed my hands on my lap, stared at the floor, and rested there in silence. I have no idea how much time had passed. I

144

didn't dare lift my gaze from the small, square tile on the floor. It had a slight fracture. Mold grew in its crack.

Suddenly, a man entered the room and the air changed.

"Helllllo, there. My name is Doctor Finnegan. I understand you are hoping for a medical abortion today."

Well, he cuts right to the chase, I thought. Oddly refreshing, no beating around the bush.

"Um, yes," was all that I could muster.

"Well, it says here that you believe yourself to be about a month along. Now, the common misconception is that you 'get pregnant' when you conceive. In reality, you have to count from your last skipped period before the date of conception. Does that make sense to you, Miss Cain?"

"I'm not... no, I don't understand. So how far along am I?"

"We're going to send you out for an ultrasound in a few minutes. That should be able to tell us exactly how far along you are because, as I'm sure you read in our forms, you cannot receive a medical abortion if you are more than ten weeks pregnant in the state of Florida."

"So, are you saying I may have to...get surgical?" My eyes stole a glance at the hidden instruments.

"If it's only been a month since you had the encounter that you believe got you pregnant, you should be fine. There can always be the surprise of it being sooner, but if you've only skipped one period, you should be able to receive a medical abortion."

"Okay... thanks."

I had no idea how to respond to anything he said.
It all felt too surreal to absorb at all.

And then as soon as he arrived, he was gone. Within five minutes, I was led out of the room into a small, dark closet. It was nearly secretive. They asked me to please keep my voice down as I approached it. I assumed it was because of the closed doors on either side. Behind them were women who were experiencing a moment meant for joy, seeing a child on that tiny screen for the first time. But in this place, it didn't elicit happy tears so much as painfully guilty ones.

A middle-aged nurse asked me to change into a hospital gown and lie down on the gurney. Once they came back in, the process was fast. The nurse informed me that if they can't register the pregnancy with an ultrasound, that it is still too early to abort and that I would need to come back in a few weeks. I must not have read the forms well enough, because that possibility made me feel ill. I was solidified in my decision to have this abortion, today. How could I walk around another few weeks allowing this baby to grow knowing what I would be doing to it?

Before I knew it, they had the ultrasound under way. The nurse asked me if I wanted to see the baby and, if not, to turn my head away from the screen for the duration of the procedure. I kept my head as far to the left as physically possible. The tendons on my neck strained. As she moved the instrument, I was praying that I was far enough along. If my religion teacher from high school could see me now, I thought, she'd be shaking her head, cursing herself for not teaching me well enough.

The nurse brought me out of my reverie with five words: I see a yolk sac. She told me that she had located the gestational sac, and that the size indicated that I was actually about six weeks along. Without realizing what I was doing, I turned my head toward her. Out of the corner of my eye, I saw it. On the screen was a tiny, black, shaded area. It was all I could make out before I snapped my head back to the other side. She finished the exam and was out the door. I was left alone in the darkness with that little, shadowy, cotton-ball of a baby. For the first time that day, I cried.

The rest of my time spent in the clinic was a haze. Seeing the image on the computer screen sent me into autopilot. I couldn't think of anything else. They brought me into a room that looked like a small lawyer's office where an older, Indian woman asked me if I was sure I wanted to have the abortion. I said yes, and she informed me that my "counseling" was now completed. That was it. Then, they brought me into another waiting area to sit with a half-dozen other women who were anticipating their different procedures. Most of the girls had no distinguishable bump. One woman was far enough along that I was amazed she was still legally allowed to terminate. She must have caught me looking because she turned to me and began to speak.

"Is this your first time?"

I was blown away by that question. Who would ever go through this more than once? I nodded.

"Don't worry, honey," she said leaning toward me "This is my fifth surgical and it's nothin'. They kinda put you out, you won't feel a thing."

I was so shocked at her nonchalant explanation that I didn't even tell her I wasn't getting a surgical procedure. Five times? I'm not proud of myself for this, but I judged her. Who could be selfish enough to terminate five pregnancies instead of using a fucking condom? But I didn't know her story, and it was wrong of me to assume what brought her to this ending. I mean, really, who was I to judge in this moment. Stones at glass houses.

Finally, I was called. I was placed on the table of that same room as I found myself in the beginning of the day, twelve, with the overwhelming lights. A different doctor stood before me, he was older and graying. He wore a frown, but he didn't look bored or tired as did the nurses I'd seen throughout the day. He looked heated. His expression betrayed not just annoyance at giving yet another woman the means to end her pregnancy, but anger. At least, that's what he demeanor conveyed to me. I felt like I was sitting before a bitter father, disgusted that his daughter would not only allow a man to violate her, but also leave her with a marker of the sin. I felt branded. I may as well have been wearing a scarlet "A" across my chest.

"Miss Cain, you have opted for a medical abortion. You will be given two pills. One is called mifepristone. It will stop the pregnancy from continuing. The other is called misoprostol. That will cause the uterus to expel the pregnancy. In accordance with Florida State law, I must hand you the first pill which you will take in this room, now, in front of me. The second pill you will take at home within the next 8 hours. If you change your mind after leaving this office, and do not take the second pill, your child will suffer severe birth defects. Do you understand what I am telling you?"

I was so intimidated by him; my mouth went dry and I couldn't answer. Luckily, a nurse had entered the room in the middle of his speech. She moved to my side and gently stroked my arm.

"Sweetheart, you have to answer before we can give you the pill. Are you okay with everything Doctor Spalding just told you?" She was so kind; I will be forever grateful for the humanity she showed me in that moment.

"Sorry, yes, I, um, I understand."

He nodded to the nurse and peeled the thin, transparent cover off of a small, plastic pill container, maybe a few centimeters in size. In a fluid movement, he placed the pill in his hand and moved it toward me. I stared at it for a moment. A legion of questions hit me at once. But every time I tried to grasp one well enough to answer it, another one stole its place. There were too many, I realized, and I doubted that would change. So, with a million parts of my mind in a symphony of uproar, I stole the pill from his palm and placed it on my tongue. The nurse offered me a small, paper-cone filled with water and, with its help, I swallowed. I felt the pill with every inch that it traveled inside of me.

Suddenly, my mind was quiet. Almost as if there was nothing else for it to fight. Before the doctor left, he gave me a plastic bottle filled with one, lone pill. It was the second pill I was meant to take "in the comfort of my home." He also gave me a prescription for hydrocodone. As he walked out he informed me that the cramps might become severe, and to use the prescription as instructed to reduce the pain. The nurse suggested I stop at a pharmacy and grab some extra-large sanitary pads. I nodded and walked out the door towards the waiting room. I felt my personal scarlet letter burning a fiery red as I joined the land of the living once again.

~

There's too much that I experienced that night to unpack here.
Phoebe drove me home.
I took the pill.
I felt the pain.

There was a moment, maybe around midnight, that I had tried to check in with myself. It was during one of the times that I had struggled to drag myself, bent over in fetal position, to the bathroom. Like a computer running a diagnostic program, I surveyed.

I had never felt more detached from myself.
People talk about out of body experiences in literature.
That feeling when your body is forced to endure something so completely terrifying to your consciousness, that your mind sort of taps out of the moment.
Adrenaline, the ego, whatever you want to call it: it takes the wheel.
And, then, the mind is saved from awareness.
You can get through it, because you have shut down the part of yourself that makes you more than just a body.
More than pale, white bones covered in thick cartilage and submerged in that slick, shimmering, deep-red blood.
For those hours, and for the first time in my entire life, I lived in the moment.
Each moment of unsteadiness, when I was sure I would faint.
Every aching, powerfully painful contraction as my body attempted to eradicate the intruder.
Because that is exactly what my body perceived the fetus as: a foreign invader.

I had created a potential new life with the man I almost married. For so many reasons, this was heartbreaking. But the most painful of all of those reasons was the knowledge that in the end, I had instructed my body to remove it. No, I had demanded it.

I never told Kurt because he'd already hurt me so much, I knew I couldn't trust him to not hurt me again. And there was just too much on the line. I couldn't risk him telling me, "No, Brett, not only do I not want to be with you, but I also want nothing to do with this child. You're going to have to be alone and also figure this out by yourself." I just didn't have it in me. And, in the end, wouldn't I wind up in the same position anyway?

As I crawled to the bathroom on my hands and knees for the fifteenth time that night, a mixture of tears and sweat pooling at the small of my neck, I realized: this wasn't all just about me. Yes, Kurt hurt me, and I would never consider being hurt that way again. But this pregnancy, this baby that was in that exact moment being torn out of me, was that the being that deserved to bare the consequence? Kurt and I had made a mistake by spending a night together. The night ended with a potential life and I had snuffed it out without so much as informing the father that it existed.

So, yes, Kurt was the villain in my story.
But if he knew what I had done,
would I become the villain in his?
Am I the villain here, no matter
whose story it was to tell?

It was all too much.
The broken promises,
the painful truths,
the feelings of emptiness and unworthiness:
they all culminated into this night
and those two little pills.

I fell onto the floor of my bathroom,
the cool tiles sliding down my back,
and I cried.

I cried for Kurt
never knowing what I did.
I cried for the baby
that I stopped from
being formed.

But, mostly, I cried
for myself,
because I knew
there was no
coming back from
this.

Yes, I would survive,
but I would never be the same.
I thought that it was painful
to have your heart broken
by a man.

Tonight, I learned that it is
much more painful
to realize that you've just
stolen the life
of your own child.

Phoebe heard my wails and she opened the bathroom door. I was bleeding heavily, and she told me that all the color had drained from my face. She pulled me up off of the floor and, as I leaned on her, she moved me to the living room and onto the brown leather sofa. That couch had been the first thing I'd seen every day when I got home from work. It was placed directly across from the door and, so many times before, Kurt would be upon it. Rolling a joint, licking the paper and as he folded it, he would smile. And my heart would feel light. Now, the couch no longer housed that warm memory. It was a place for me to gain my strength through all of this pain. She sat me down in its middle. Slowly, I raised my legs to stretch out against its cool rawhide. I laid my head down to allow the leather to chill my sweat-covered skin. I would never look at this couch and remember anything but this feeling of helplessness.

Did I make a mistake?
I questioned myself.
Does it matter now?
I felt myself answer back.

CHAPTER 18

The next morning, I awoke to the smell of coffee. As my sleep-drunk nose followed the scent, I glanced into the kitchen. Phoebe was brewing a small pot, just enough for two little cups. Standing in the sunlit, bare window facing the street, she was glowing. Incandescent. To me, she'd been facing the light in such a way lately that it made her appear illuminated. She probably always did that, I thought to myself. She was simply standing in a sunbeam. She would have laughed at me and told me, playfully, to shut the fuck up if I ever told her. I think it was because she truly had been my own personal angel these past few months, as trite as it sounded.

Trying to figure out life as an only child had always been particularly difficult for me. It was lonely, and living life without an older role model or someone younger I needed to look out for left me feeling like I was constantly without purpose. It would have been a beautiful thing to be an older sister to Morris. Just not in the cards. But ever since I met Phoebe, I enjoyed a sense of more than just purpose. I basked in community. Beyond that, even, I felt that sense of sibling connection I'd always longed for. No matter what, we had each other's back. And, shit, did she show up for me.

Turning my way and seeing that I was up, Phoebe slowly walked with soft steps towards me. She placed the cups of coffee down, fragrant and filled to the brim, and sat in the chair next the bed. Her hand placed delicately on mine; she cracked a hesitant smile.

"How are you feeling? Your colour looks better."

"I feel okay. Tired, but good. What time did I finally go to bed?"

"Oh, maybe four? It was a long night," she yawned, unwillingly.

"Ah," I said shifting my aching body slightly. "Shit, you must be exhausted. Tell me you at least slept when I did."

"I was worried something would happen to you while you slept…"

"Pheebs!" I cut her off. "Ugh, you shouldn't have done that. You need to sleep, man. Look, I feel good enough to go grab some food. What do you want?"

"Are you sure?" She asked, wearily. You've, um, lost a lot of… you may need more time to recover, Brett."

"No, trust me, I need out of here. Fresh air will be nice, anyways. I'll run up to that Asian place in downtown. I'm craving bubble tea."

"Okay, I can come with you?" She was already standing to retrieve her purse.

"No way, dude, you need to sleep. Plus, I need you awake later to help me research a new place. I don't think I can stay here any longer…" I stole a quick glance at the bathroom.

"Do you maybe want to… talk before you head out? I know that there must be a lot going on in your mind right now. Maybe it would help?"

"Who are you, Dr. Phil?" I asked playfully budging her arm. "Really, I'm fine, Pheebs. Just need some sushi."

I changed absentmindedly, grabbed my purse and stopped to glance into the mirror on the way out. I quickly understood why she was so concerned with how my inner health – my outer appearance was shocking. I had knots in my hair, my makeup from the day before was smeared and my clothes were hanging off of my body as if they were two sizes too big. I was not the picture of a human being at all, let alone a healthy one. Moving closer to the reflective glass, I attempted to fix some of the mess. Meeting my own gaze, I felt a small shiver creep up my spine.

I did not see a woman who had grown stronger and more protective of herself. I didn't see a woman hardened by her experiences nor broken by the harsh reality of the past few months. In the mirror looking back at me was the 10-year-old version of myself. I saw the naivete, the unsureness, the fear. It was as if I had regressed nearly two decades overnight. The little girl staring back at me was begging for a do-over. I whispered a silent apology to her as I turned away and walked out the door, firmly shutting it behind me.

~

Locking my car after I parked outside of the restaurant, I walked out of the garage and onto the sidewalk. It was a gorgeous day. Bright. Sunny. I wanted so badly to feel the breeze on my face, to allow that fresh feeling to wash away the past few nights. I'd been so busy trying to survive the past twelve hours that I'd buried the night before.

Tom.

Just thinking his name made me shake my head hastily in an attempt to brush off everything that was attached to it now.

Walking into the restaurant, I felt my stomach turn. Waiting in line to order, I realized that I knew about this spot because Lana and Tom had taken me here just a few weeks ago. Paying for my take-out, I recalled how we'd dined on fresh sushi and savory pho. As I waited for the food near the counter, I remembered how we'd laughed about the night we'd met and how Lana had nearly beat a guy up for me. We must have looked like we had known each other for years. I wanted that to be true. After the break-up, I needed to find friends who would help usher me into singledom with light drinks and heavy laughs. Instead, I met people who had a soft spot for fake friendships, hard drugs and drunken assault.

Still, I stayed lost in that memory. Minutes must have passed, and I was shaken out of that reverie when I heard my name being called by the woman who took my order. Embarrassed and red-faced, I walked up quickly to retrieve the food. I whispered an all-too-quiet apology as she handed it off. I don't know why I had felt so self-conscious lately.

The woman must have been naturally kind. Warm, like the sun that day. She recognized my timid demeanor and said, brightly, and with encouragement, "Hey, no problem, girl. We all get lost up in there sometimes." She tapped an index finger to her head as she spoke those last few words. I smiled, a thin pull on the corners of my lips. So true, I thought, that getting lost in your own thoughts is universal. It was a subtle reminder; one she would probably forget she passed on to me in less than a minute. But it made me feel seen, and it stuck with me for the rest of my life.

Once I had my food in hand, I didn't even take a moment to make sure that my order was correct. I just wanted to leave downtown and get back home. But the thought of that made me feel worse: I didn't want that to be my home, either. I'd lived in Orlando my whole life. Maybe it was time for a change. I have friends everywhere, I told myself. I was reminded of that just a few weeks ago. I can't believe I ever let myself forget it in the first place. I'd be fine to start somewhere new. Yes, I'd just gotten that promotion, but Cheryl could just as easily transfer me to another office. We had plenty, and luckily most were far from here. Fuck, I realized. I was stuck in thought again. How did people turn this off? How many roses did I have to stop and smell before I could be deemed a "live in the now" type of person?

I was deeply down yet another rabbit hole when I heard my name being called. It was coming from a table near me. When I turned my head, I noticed the unmistakably striking good looks of none other than Luke.

Oh wow,

Luke.

He looked just as handsome as always and seeing him made me smile with some natural happiness of which I'd forgotten I was even capable. I wrote him off too quickly, I thought to myself. Lots of people date multiple people at once. Hell, I could have learned a lot from him. Confidence, carpe diem. Maybe I should ask him to go out for drinks one night soon. It was in that moment that he sat back in his chair just enough to reveal who was with sitting in the chair next to him, sparkling like a jewel. Gita, that gorgeous, exotically addicting woman. She waved me over to their table. Like a moth to a flame once again, I began walking towards them. Only then did I realize who was coming up behind me to sit down at that table, across from them.

"Brett, heeeeeyyyy, girl!" Lana said through strained lips.

I froze. I was too close to walk away without saying something. Stuttering, I forced myself to speak.

"W-wow, hey. Its, uh, been a while. What's up, guys?"

Luke looked at me, and then at Lana. He had a confused look on his face, like he was in the middle of an inside joke and wanted to know what was so funny. Then, I noticed the person who was about to sit next to Lana. Falling into the chair, Tom didn't look up. He merely stared at his phone, removing himself from the commotion. Good, I thought, as I stared at the side of his face.

Look at me and I swear I'll tear you apart.

"Trouble, it's been a while. How have you been?" Luke inquired with a casual sip of his drink.

With that question, Lana turned towards me and stared at me. The look in her eyes could have burned a hole in a brick wall, and I knew it was a warning.

"Yeah, been busy. Work, you know."

"Well don't be a stranger. Gita and I were telling these two to come out with us next weekend. I've got some friends coming into town, sort of a college reunion. They're fun guys and I'm sure they'd love to meet you and any single friends you may have hidden," he said playfully bumping into Gita. She laughed, mockingly and grabbed his thigh with a gentle squeeze. Wow, so that's what it must be like. To feel free and weightless.

"Yeah, I'll let you know. Good seeing you guys."

With that I turned and walked towards the door. I had never begged my feet to move more quickly in my entire life. But they felt heavy, like in a dream when you're running from a monster, but your feet are trudging through quicksand. Agonizing over this heaviness, I felt a hint of vertigo approaching. I had lost a lot of blood. Maybe this was too much too fast? I needed to go home, lie down with Pheebs, and watch shitty show for the rest of the day. Was *Desperate Housewives* still on TV?

Just as I was reaching the exit, I felt a hand on my shoulder. I turned around to see Lana standing before me, a calm and nearly timid smile lay across her face.

"Look, Brett, about what happened…"

I was floored. Knowing Lana, she liked to ignore the things that weren't helpful to her reputation. I assumed a boyfriend who moonlighted as a predator would have been high on the list of things to pretend didn't exist. I knew she had nothing to apologize for, but still, it felt good to have it addressed. Everyone ignoring what happened to me would have been painful. I had to let her know I didn't hold anything against her. It wasn't her fault.

"Yeah, Lana I don't want you to feel—"

"What? Annoyed that you went after my boyfriend? Disgusted that you thought you could try and make a move when he was hammered? You know what, Brett, you really are a piece of work. I expect this shit from the typical downtown street rats. I mean, I get that Tom is desirable. He's got a good job, comes from a good family. I wouldn't be dating him if I didn't see that. But, *really,* waiting until I wasn't around to try and tell him how

158

you feel? Oldest trick in the book. And don't think you're the first girl to try this shit with him. I don't understand why you bitches can't just stay away and let us be happy. No wonder your marriage didn't work out. Really, fuck you, Brett. I thought I could trust you, but you're just like every girl. Don't contact *any* of us again. I mean it."

I stood there, food in hand, totally and completely frozen. As she left to turn back to her table, she replaced that angry expression with her typical smile. That forced, trying to keep up the act, look.

"Bye, girl! See you next weekend!"

I couldn't speak, I couldn't think. I was too shaken up by what had just happened. She was telling me that Tom did nothing wrong. Jesus, she was telling *herself* that. In fact, she had convinced herself that he did nothing to me at all. He was just a victim of my "female gaze" and I was the whore who wanted to get with her boyfriend. I was mad about that, obviously. But even more infuriating, no, *sickening*, was how she had said that I wasn't "the first girl." Had he done this before to other women? Was he a predator that waited in the shadows for a girl wasted on sadness and shitty liquor to make the mistake of allowing herself to be alone with him? It sent shivers down my spine to think I wasn't the only girl who had to shower away the feeling of being assaulted by him. His rough hands. Again, I shook myself to allow the memory of that night to fall off of me, only to drip down my chest and settle, marinating, in my stomach until it shot back up to rear its ugly head in my mind once again.

Before I turned around to walk out the door and back to my car, I saw Luke wave to me.

His big arms, the ones that had been around my body not so long ago, curled in one fluid motion across the gorgeously tanned shoulders of Gita. She smiled and coiled herself into him. Grabbing Gita's hand from across the table, Lana laughed, loudly and boastfully. The little voice in my head that had become so timid assured me that they were laughing at me.

Tom sat quietly next to Lana. Eyes down, he appeared almost embarrassed. Good. Guilt. It was small, but it was something. At least he felt bad for what he did. Then, I watched him slowly move his hand to sit on top of Lana's. Immediately, she drew it back out and threw it in the air, boldly expressing along with her story. Maybe not obvious to the others, but in that moment, I knew. He doesn't feel bad for what he did to *me*, he's just making sure he doesn't get into trouble with *her*.

~

As I pulled back into my driveway, the heaviness of the past forty-eight hours loomed over me. Like a dark, heavy cloud waiting to unload its haul, it surrounded me entirely. I felt its presence; I recognized its desire to release. But I couldn't let it unburden itself upon me. It wasn't that I was fighting back tears; I've never been one to excel in that category. I genuinely felt as though it wasn't my weight to bear. All the heaviness, I didn't feel connected to it anymore. I merely shrugged it off and assumed the clouds would materialize elsewhere.

Truthfully, I didn't feel connected to *me*, anymore, either.

Walking through the doors, I heard the shower running. Phoebe was notorious for her long showers: one day, in college, she asked to shower at our place because, supposedly, she liked our water pressure better. She spent a solid forty-five minutes in there. I found out later that year that Phoebe had been *forced* out because her roommates put time limits on her, and she wasn't too happy about that. So, I knew she'd be in there for a while.

I unloaded our food, set up the plates and cutlery, and tried to start eating. I took one bite. Again. Sandpaper. The sensation of chewing felt like I was ripping apart extra-dry jerky covered in extremely thick peanut butter. I set down my fork. Then, I heard a phone buzz. I searched for my cell in my purse. Pulling it out, I saw I had no new notifications. I heard the buzz go off again. The little phone to my right was lighting up. The cover was a turquoise blue. Phoebe's. I glanced over at the screen.

The name across its glass face made my heart stop.

Kurt.

Going through someone else's phone without their permission was wrong, and I knew that. But seeing his name, I couldn't even stop my hand from reaching for the little metal rectangle.

Kurt.

The name that echoed through my mind every day since he left. The name I cursed and praised. I slid open the lock on her phone. All I saw were two texts in their message chain.

Phoebe:

> okay, and you know how much I care about you.
> But now one of us has to tell her,
> and I really think it should be you.

Kurt:

> I don't even know how to do that, Pheebs.
> I've hurt her enough already by lying.
> Maybe she doesn't have to find out just yet.

My head was racing.
Is this what I thought it was?
No, I told myself.
I was just jumping to conclusions.
It looked bad,
but it couldn't be what my mind was screaming at me
at the top of its lungs.
They're together.
Phoebe and Kurt.

No, no way.

But what else could that have meant?

How long had this been going on?

Was she... ?

No.

No.

I had to stop myself. I needed to ask Kurt first before I said anything to Phoebe. Immediately, I pulled out my phone and searched for his number. Pulling Kurt into a text conversation, I typed out what I wanted to say as calmly as I possibly could. Unfortunately, that was easier said than done.

Brett:

What did I just see on Phoebe's phone, Kurt?
Tell me I'm wrong,
tell me she isn't the one you left me for.
The one who you wrote that poem about.
Tell me you aren't with Phoebe.

I waited. I still heard the shower running. I begged her to be taking the longest shower of her life. I needed to hear it from him, before I heard it from her.

No.

There's just no way.

Was there?

I stopped myself. There was nothing to hear. They had been friends for as long as I'd known either of them. Phoebe had a boyfriend for years. Seth. He'd been struggling. She'd been texting him every time I was with her.

That was *him* she was texting, right?

Or has it been *Kurt* this whole time?

My mind was racing. Completely unbridled, I had found myself waiting back in limbo. But this time, I truly wished I had stayed in the dark. The light brought with it an answer that I wasn't sure I could handle. For a few minutes, there was nothing.

Nothing.

Just the sound of a mental thunderstorm and questions spinning in my head. Then, I felt a buzz. It was him. Turning over the phone in my hand, I took a deep breath. I knew that when I slid my finger across the screen to unlock it, an answer to a question I'd been asking myself for months would be there, across the screen in small black letters.

I'd never wanted to be wrong more in my entire life.

Kurt:

> Brett, I don't know what to say.
> I'm so sorry.
> I didn't want you to find out this way.
> Don't blame her, please.

So that was it.

All along,

It had been her.

It had been Phoebe.

CHAPTER 19

I felt the room cave in.

It was big
and then it was
small.

Then it was
sideways,
and suddenly
I was thrown into a
rabbit hole.

Down and down
I went,
a true Alice,
suffering from a
total and complete
change in myself.

The life I'd known, the world all my own, had been thrown out the
door for months, now. But, somehow, it had never felt more nonsensical

than it did now. I heard the shower handle pull, and the light downpour of water end. Suddenly, Phoebe stood before me. She smiled as she moved, wrapped in a towel, to the bed to put on her clothes. I waited for her to finish. As she moved towards me to sit at her plate of Asian dumplings, I sat, dazed and dumb.

She must have realized that my quiet meant something was wrong. Instinctively, she tried to fix it, like she'd done so many times before.

"Hey, I have an idea. Let's watch a shitty show. I think they have *Desperate Housewives* on here somewhere," she said as she fumbled with the TV remote.

Wow, look at that, I thought bitterly. Two peas in a fucking pod. As she continued to search I sat silently and watched her. Yes, I was mad. More than that, I was amazed. I was amazed that she was able to hide this from me.

How did she do it?

I mean, truly, *how?*

She was there for me the day after the breakup. She drove all the way to Orlando to make sure that I was okay. She watched me open the door with bloodshot eyes. She sat with me, cried with me. She kept me company while I contacted people to tell them that the wedding was called off. She told me, with fire in her eyes, that he was a jerk and that I deserved so much better. Jesus, she brought me to the clinic as I decided to abort his *child*.

It was sick, it was all so fucking sick.

Finally, I couldn't take it anymore. I asked her the only question I could think of in that moment. Completely emotionless, I let the words fall out.

"Phoebe, how could you?"

165

She looked at me with total confusion, a slight smile garnishing her face. I had said it so monotone that she must have thought that I was messing with her. That I was trying to institute some teasing roleplay. We had always peppered our friendship with constant insults and a tirade of teasing. We were never fond of "girly" friendships. We found in one another the perfect mirror image. Complimented each other like colors. All we ever wanted from each other was someone to appreciate without having to say so. So, commonly, "I love you" came out as "fuck you." Thus, she was waiting for the prank to make sense. It was only when she saw the pain in my eyes that she realized: I wasn't joking.

"Oh, God, Brett. Um, okay, just hear me out…"

"Get out."

"Brett, no, listen. You need to hear my side of this, please, you—"

"Phoebe, there is—and I mean this—nothing you could ever say to me ever again to make me understand why you would do this. I mean, how *could* you, Pheebs?!"

She was speaking, blurting out useless words to befall deaf ears. I was taking in nothing. Not one crocodile-tear-infused syllable. I just stared at her. Her body language told me she was pleading. I watched her continue trying to justify herself, attempting to tell me that she never meant to hurt me. That I, oh, yes, *I* was the one whom she would never want to hurt.

I couldn't look at her anymore. My anger was fading, and all I felt was the bitter, acute pain of betrayal. Yes, Kurt broke my heart. With time, fixable. Then, Tom preyed on the pieces of it. Sure, more jagged but, again, fixable. Yeah, the clinic stomped those pieces into bits of dust. A tiny, miniscule powder. But I was still on the floor, knees aching, attempting to pool that dust into a pile with my fingers. I could still scoop that up. Store it somewhere safe. But, Phoebe? Well, she had just shoveled those pulverized fragments up off the floor and, in one giant breath, sent them scattering. She had been holding the strings to all of this, everything, the whole time. A puppet-master. It was truly a talent, hiding behind the scenes, playing innocent.

My best friend and my fiancé had an affair.

All these years, I leaned on you, I thought. You were the person. *My* person. Now, you are just the missing piece of this disaster of a puzzle I had been trying to solve since the night of my twenty-sixth birthday.

I'd finally solved it, and now, now I could throw it away.
I tuned back into her words, just long enough.

"Okay, okay, I know I fucked up, I know I did but, *Brett,* you don't *understand.* Its *Kurt,* and I knew that if I told you, you wouldn't see—"
"Jesus, *no,* Phoebe. I'm not *listening* to this! After everything, *everything* I have been through. LEAVE, NOW!"
Phoebe looked at me with pain in her eyes. When I gazed at her, all I saw was a stranger. Tears welling up in her eyes to replace the ones already falling, she moved to pick up her bag. She gathered her things quickly, moving like an animal fearing for its life. Finally, walking towards the door, she turned towards me. She opened her mouth to speak, but no sound escaped her lips. And then, she was gone.

~

I had been here before. But this time was harder.
Alone.

I was alone.
And the pain was unbearable.
and so, we beat on

Tears.

All the tears of the past few months engulfed me in one moment.

I loved Kurt, God, did I love him.

Kurt.
His notebook.
The Poem.
An Unsent Letter.

Phoebe… There was no fix for this.

No fix.

Who do I call for this heartbreak?

No one to call.
Not really.
No fix.

Nothing.

But there was always an escape.
The pills.
They won't leave.
A full bottle.

Just two –
maybe, maybe
four this time.

Time: it's a funny thing, isn't it?
How long has it been since…

Phoebe, *why*?
It fucking hurts.
Everything does.

Long enough for another one?

Sure.

One, two

So tiny,
these little
yellow dots.

Fuck, it was her.
How long?

I don't want to feel this one.

Every book
Has an ending

Doesn't it?

Finished.

Three more,
A sip of water.

T   I   M   E

A flash.
        The

                corner of my eye.

The mirror.

The girl in it.
                The Yellow Wallpaper.
                        The girl.

I've left her alone in it t o o   l o n g.

C r a s h.

There.
Now you can be

r e l e a s e d ,   too.

D o   oo oooo w n

                                                    a

                                                    n

                                                    d

                d oooowwnn

                        I go.

I t   t a k e s

all the running

y o u   c a n

dooooooo

to

S   t   a   yyyy

　　　　　　　　in the   s aaaameeee pl a   c e.

F i na ll y.

Just

D r e   a m in g

About

　　　　　　　　　　　　　Th e

　　　　　　lions.

Fading.
A door creaks.

A thud.

Two hands
cradle the sides of my face.

Her voice.

"Brett, stay
with
me"

Then,

                  darkness.

AN ANSWER

wish I could know how much time has passed now. It feels like years, but it can't have been more than just a couple of days. Painfully long days stretched to the point of obscurity. When you are lying flat on your back, eyes sealed to the world, entombed in a chamber of burning white light, time becomes merely a suggestion.

All I know is that I am still here,
but, now,
now I remember why.

It's a strange feeling, dying. Some people have used the euphemism, "circling the drain". I always wondered how that came to be a metaphor. I picture when a child drops a coin in those fancy donation devices, the kind that forces it into a universe-type cyclone. The coin continually orbits the funnel with broad circles that gradually become smaller and smaller. I used to feel oddly about those contraptions. They always seemed so torturous. The coin is unaware that with each massive revolution, they are actually coming closer and closer to being sucked into oblivion.

That is what lying here feels like.
With each passing instant,

my moments of living become smaller and smaller.

My breaths feel more forced.

My soul feels like it's being pulled into obscurity.

Someone comes into my room. I feel their fingertips delicately trace the skin above my eyebrow, as if I am made of butterfly wings. Now, their breath is in my ear, warm and soft. All I hear are three words. Faint.

"I'm so sorry."

Kurt.

Now I know.

How could you?

How could either of you?

He sits. I hear the quiet settling of a body into metal. Tears being stifled. Then, he speaks.

"I am so, so sorry. I … did this. *Fuck.*"

No more words for a moment. Did the room get smaller? When you find yourself with an excessive amount of time on your hands, your mind wanders. I have found myself tormented with this curse.

Moments pass. Maybe days? No, just moments. This experience is proving to me something that crossed my mind any time I got high: time is a construct. At times, it is moving at a snail's pace. At others, it rips through at light-speed.

Time.

Again, he speaks.

"I didn't know how to tell you. *God*, I should have just told you. I mean, shit, I didn't even know. Not really, I guess."

You didn't know?
That you loved her?
How long until you both figured it out?
"It was just, friendship, I thought. We were always so close, since high school."

High school?
No, that's not right.
You didn't know each other in high school.

"It's his fault! He shouldn't have told me how he felt, it was… confusing and, honestly, I didn't even want to admit it to myself, even when I knew."

His fault?
He?
Oh, my god.
I made a mistake.

"I loved Jay, Brett. *Fuck*, I *loved* him. And he just, he just *left* me. And now, and now look what happened."

Jay.
Jay.
       My god,
           it was Jay.

The poems.
The truth that ruined everything.

The Unsent Letter.

It all makes sense.
Oh, god.
What have I done?

"I can't even blame him. It's all my fault. Brett, *God*, Brett. I'm so sorry that I let you believe it was Phoebe. I didn't know how to admit it to myself. He was gone and I figured that was it. But he never left my mind. And I didn't know how to... God, I am *so*, so sorry."

Tears.
The whole room is flooded.
A door opens.
It shuts.

I was wrong.

~

I notice a change. New fluids must have been added to my IV. My veins send an ice-cold sensation through the highways that lay beneath my skin. I feel like my insides are being refrigerated. Like I'm fresh meat being preserved for a later date of consumption. I wonder what my expiration date is.

Please, I need more time.
I was wrong.
I can fix this.
I *need* to fix this.

Fix.

~

Someone has just entered.
I hear a door shut, quietly.
They walk up to my bed.
Slow steps, shuffles.

Then, a light tug on the tubes in my hand. It must be a nurse. I hear her mention to someone that there has been no change, that I am still deep in my coma.

"Thank you," I hear.

Phoebe.
Oh, Phoebe.
I am *so* sorry.

For a while, nothing is said.
I hear her shift her weight as she stands by my side.
Always by my side.

"I know I should have told you. What we were talking about."

She sounds apologetic.
Why isn't she mad at me?

"I started texting him about this. About you. God, maybe a few weeks ago? I just... you were scaring me. All the partying and drugs. And then the..."

I know.
The pills.

"I just knew you were circling it, Brett. I needed some reinforcements. I couldn't tell your parents. By the way, they're on their way. Flying down from North Carolina. I don't even want to tell you how upset they are right now. They love you so much…"

Mom.
Dad.
I'm so sorry.

"I needed him to know what was going on with you. What he caused. I needed to know why he left you. I promised, anything he told me, it wouldn't get back to you. And then, he told me. It took him forever, I practically had to get him there myself. For him to realize." A little chuckle.

You're sad.
I'm sorry.

"Then it all made so much sense. *Jay*. I kind of always got a feeling about Jay. I think he just *really*, really loved Kurt, you know? I don't know that he ever realized he was *in love* with him. Maybe that was why he left? I guess we would know if we ever read those notes, right?"

He left.
We never knew why.
This makes sense.
How did I not see it?

"Anyways, I promised Kurt I wouldn't tell you. Even after he got you… even after the clinic. I begged him to tell you. That's what you saw, I guess. Me asking him to be honest with you. You deserved that. I never told him about that day, just so you know."

Loyal until the end.

I'm sorry, Phoebe.

"I just... how could you do this, Brett? *Why*? How am I," she says, choking back tears, "how am I supposed to do this without you? You're my *best friend*."

You're mine, too.

Always.

And with that, she places her hand in mine.

So small.

In a force of strength, all I can muster,

my hand squeezes hers.

Once.

Tightly.

And then,

"Hi, Morris."

AFTERWORD

t would have been nice for this book to end in happiness. With love. With communication. With forgiveness. It would have felt good to turn the final page and know that everyone got the ending they deserved. That happiness, true happiness, isn't a construct.

But this isn't that story.
And this isn't that ending.

Brett's life ended in misery, in wasted talent and possibility. Her paper world dissolved like all those lies and misunderstandings she held onto. Melted to nothing like the smallest puddle of water. This isn't a feel-good story about destiny.

This is a pile of rubble
that didn't stop stacking
on a woman who couldn't see

what was right in front of her.

If you or someone you know needs help,
you can find help at the Crisis Text Line
and the Suicide Prevention Lifeline.
They are free and available to talk 24/7:

Text "Hello" to the Crisis Text Line at 741741
Call the Lifeline at 1-800-273-8255

ACKNOWLEDGEMENTS

I am lucky. I have so many people to thank, and I know it. Always.

Thank you to my incredible cover designers – Jordan Estefan and Lindsay Yates. I don't understand art, so what you two created really is a masterpiece to me.

To my parents, Jan and Marty. Thank you will never encompass how much I owe you both. You have given me the most incredible life anyone could ask for. You have celebrated me, spoiled me, loved me, taught me humility, taught me strength. You've both shown me what it means to be a good human being. I truly owe everything, including this book, to you both.

To my husband, Kyle. You have been my tether more often than I give you credit. Thank you for being my guiding light, even in my darkest hours. Thank you for picking me up off the floor when I feel shattered into pieces. Thank you for celebrating life's highs with me. And thank you for stealing me away to Canada with you – you are always the best journey I have ever taken. I cannot wait for us to be parents. I love you, 5ever.

To my best friend, Casey. You saved my life; I need you to know that. If I hadn't had your friendship through my hardest years, I wouldn't be here today. You are the sister I got to choose, and I love you with my entire heart. And to our uniquely weird college group. I couldn't have gotten through these past ten years without you all. Ten years? Aren't we all still eighteen? Thank you for helping me grow into the person I am today.

And to my guardian angel, Bakka. I was lucky enough to spend 22 years with you, Bakka, my best friend. You always were my biggest cheerleader. Thank you for putting me in my place when I needed it. I promise to hear, but not listen. I love you, again and again.

And to Walter. I would have loved to have guided you through life as your big sister. Hell, you probably would have taught me more than I taught you. One day, and I truly believe this, we will meet. And I will hold you and protect you for the rest of eternity.

ABOUT THE AUTHOR

Maureen Cummins Stinson lives in Georgina, Ontario. She lives on Lake Simcoe with her husband, Kyle, their son, Myles, and their three cats. Although she currently lives in Canada, she is originally American born and bred. Maureen was born in Orlando, Florida and lived there most of her life. She went to Florida State University and studied English Literature, with an emphasis in Shakespeare. She is a certified English teacher and is working on a career in publishing.

This is her debut novel.